Blitzkrieg Love

Livia Olteano

CRIMSON
ROMANCE
F+W Media, Inc.

This edition published by
Crimson Romance
an imprint of F+W Media, Inc.
10151 Carver Road, Suite 200
Blue Ash, Ohio 45242
www.crimsonromance.com

ISBN 10: 1-4405-6907-X
ISBN 13: 978-1-4405-6907-4
eISBN 10: 1-4405-6908-8
eISBN 13: 978-1-4405-6908-1

Chapter 1

"Bea, you're up."

I sighed. "Okay, Tony. Thanks."

He didn't reply. Maybe he didn't even hear—it was hard to over the loud banging of that travesty they called music. I set the costume in order and applied more shadows around my mask. Terri dragged her feet into the changing room just as I was about to leave.

"Hey, honey. They're all yours. Watch out for those preppy bastards in the corner booth—they tried to cop a feel when I walked by."

I snorted. "I'm good at crunching groins with my sexy shoes."

"Lovely. Holler if you go ahead with it."

I chuckled. "No prob. See you later."

The club was dark and music pounded like an infection. I strutted to the dancing cube and curved my spine to the best of its abilities. Dancing was my pleasure, and I loved the high that came with it. Even with that horrible banging they called music. I closed my eyes, shut down my mind, and just gave free rein to my body. It swayed to the beat, and I shook my moneymaker until muscles got sore. Time flew by when I danced. I blinked my eyes closed when it started and blinked them back open hours later when it was all done. The amount of noise actually made it easy to tear away from myself.

Dancing could bring a pleasant power surge if I did it right. The simple fact I gave myself over to the beat awakened a special part of me. It nourished a starving part of my soul, caressed and delighted something I couldn't reach otherwise. I needed my dancing high as badly as I needed to breathe. Maybe more.

There were those in the club who ignored dancers. For some of them we became moving furniture—functional and pretty to look at but not overly interesting. But there were those who absorbed our every move. We called them fans more as a joke. But if I paid attention to them as I danced, I noticed it wasn't so much a joke. The way their eyes sucked in my every move, the doe-eyed stare was a dead giveaway. They were as lost to my dancing as I was to the music driving me. It was an intimate sort of pleasure yet you shared it with everyone else there. A double-edged sword, a pleasure to look at but useless to crave. Fans danced with me on that edge of the sword every night. They lost a bit of their souls to me as I lost a bit of mine to the music, then shared the wonderfully replenishing joy of those moments together. Having fans was my real high, most likely. They gave me something no one else ever would be able to—hunger and attention from a safe distance.

And when you had fans, you had power. Dancers could use that power to keep jobs for a lot longer than their club's owners might have liked. I'd been hanging on to my cube for months already. It was all thanks to my fans. A couple of them in particular who spent obscene amounts of money each night while I danced. That hunger of theirs, that yearning and their enjoyment in being denied was my real moneymaker, not just my personal salvation but also that of my job. I didn't strip, but some of the dancers did. They were willing to give more of themselves than I could. I envied them for that generosity, imagined how the energy buzzed between them and their fans. What a rush that must have been, I thought.

We were unsung heroes of the night, taking away the horror of everyday jobs and pesky personal or family issues. The Pearl was something of a sacred ground, our source of common absolution.

We shed our fears, our inhibitions and forgot the burden of daily lives. We enjoyed, admired, worshipped even with writhing bodies and hungry eyes. At the end of the night we let go of our absolution, suspend it until next time we attended the service. Dancers were close to priests and priestesses, maybe—we served in the night rituals of lost souls. Our weapons were costumes, masks, heavy makeup, and wigs. We were heroes in disguise, even if we stripped bare. Our fans could enjoy us without worrying we'd meet face to face at the bank or on the subway. We were their nameless, faceless fantasies come true, their one-night absolutions. And they were ours.

I thrived on that power vibe. I played with it, focused on my top fans as I danced. Swayed more, worked my body harder for them and made sure they'd feel it was a gift for their loyalty. At the end I'd blow them a kiss and they'd clap. Dancing was the sweetest high I'd known, but it came with a sour downside. Once I got home and there was no audience to please, my body almost went into shock. That power exchange that kept my nerves sparkling with life died away and left me an empty shell. Until next time, when my fans would fill me with life for a precious while. It was the strongest sort of chemistry I'd ever felt, the worst kind of drug. And I was hopelessly addicted.

By the time my dance was over, I had sore feet, sore muscles in places one should never be sore, and a raging headache. I blew my high-roller fans a kiss and they clapped. The complimentary bottle of Cristal waited in the dressing room. So a regular night, all in all.

I changed quickly, got my huge bag, and braved the night air waiting for the cab. Sometimes, like any drug, dancing tempted me to go for more. I could go into moderate stripping routines like Sam was pushing for. My fanbase would probably grow. The power vibe would become stronger, but different. Baser, bluntly explicit—like their instincts as they watched me. No, I wasn't ready for that kind of vibe. I wasn't ready to give quite that much. Not yet—maybe not ever. Right now I was the mystery that tingled down their spines but didn't fully reach their groins. I liked that visual. I found comfort in the notion they yearned for more, that they'd always be left yearning for more. That they'd never get it. Denying was almost as powerful as giving.

I leaned back against the brick wall in the side alley. No cabby in sight yet, so I pulled out a cig. Drawing in deep gulps of smoke brought me down from the high a bit. A few guys were arguing in front of the Pearl. From where I stood, I could hear the crunch of punches and shouts growing louder. Some chicks joined the punch-fest, screaming or cheering on. I sighed and blew out a lungful of smoke. Life was such a miserable thing as soon as I stepped out of that changing cabin. Sometimes I felt like I was reliving the same day over and over again. It wasn't boredom that I felt out here—more like a soul-crushing desolation. Coming down from the high sucked. If I had my way, I'd never stop dancing, getting drunk on the admiration of my fans and the pleasure of denying them any sort of completion to those fleshly desires.

"Hey, kiddo."

Tony came out clutching a cig between his lips. He always had one, lit or not. Like part of his outfit or something—a trademark cig that flopped from his lips.

"Cab still not here?" he asked, frowning.

I shrugged. "He'll show. I don't mind having the time to smoke until he does."

He lit and dragged in a couple of smokes. I liked hanging out with Tony because to him silence wasn't ever awkward. You could drink with him the same way. He'd just sit there and *be*, no pressure to perform any pleasantries. Small talk was one of those obscenely overrated things in life—like getting up in the morning and drinking decaf. I found no point at all to getting up except some strong, delicious coffee, the dark nectar of the gods. No point except to get ready for the nights of dancing, that was.

"So, Sam wants you to come up with another costume for next month."

Speak of the devil. Sam had turned down my request to dance every night—he'd denied me more of my cure for the soul. He thought dancers were like lovers—you needed a bit of longing to fully appreciate them and too much of a good thing turned it sour.

I looked up at Tony and flicked some ash off my liberty stick.

"But this one is just a couple weeks old."

He shrugged. "Looks good to me, but it's up to Sam. Says you sure can afford it with all those high-rollers making gooey eyes at you."

Damn that bastard Sam. Getting new costumes was expensive, and my fans didn't send tips. Or, more accurately, I didn't take them a couple of times so they stopped trying. Taking that money from them would make me feel pressured into performing more, into returning the favor. It was a slippery slope. It might help push me into undressing before I was actually ready to give that much, slowly but steadily ruining my one true haven. There was a dress code for costumes, not too showy but showy enough. It couldn't be some sparkly lingerie; it had to be more on the burlesque side and all original for each of us. They were such a drag to get. Sam and his artful costumes would cost me rent someday. All part of his plan, no doubt.

"What the hell am I supposed to come up with now? I'm the only one who changes the damn things as often as pages in the freaking calendar."

He spat to his side and took another drag. When he looked back his eyes seemed tired, almost as tired as I felt. There was something about him that seemed familiar to me, more than a year's worth of knowing him could explain. I couldn't put my finger on it, but it was a familiarity I both enjoyed and dreaded.

"Most of the girls do their own, mix and match parts of the old ones."

I raised an eyebrow. "Do I look like I can put together a costume?"

"Do they?" he answered, grinning.

And yet they did, obviously. He had me there. Maybe I could get Terri to teach me how to do it, but I'd still have to come up with the design and crap. If I'd had fantasies of being a costume designer, I wouldn't be dancing in Sam's club. There were fancier places to dance, I was fully aware. But Sam was the first one to let me take a stab at it without any prior experience. I was grateful to the bastard.

"I'd be better off turning tricks," I grumbled.

That one had been a very hush-hush job offer from Sam something like six months ago. I'd have a sure audience, he said. He could guarantee I'd make enough to buy myself a place instead of renting a crappy one. If the stripping had been a no, turning tricks had been a hell no. I sure as hell couldn't give that much.

Tony watched me for a while, assessing. Then he shook his head.

"Don't give in to Sam's crap. You're not cut out for that shit, kiddo. Stick to dancing, trust me."

"I'm not a kid. You do know that, right? I'm twenty-two. There's a lot of younger meat turning tricks."

He smiled. "Not cut out for it. Otherwise you'd already be doing it."

He had me there. My usual cabbie finally showed up and flashed lights. "Thanks for hanging out with me while I waited."

He frowned. "I wasn't hanging, just having a smoke."

"Could have fooled me. Night, Tony."

"Think about that new costume, okay?"

I climbed in the back of the cab and slumped into the seat. My bones were tired in a way no amount of sleep would soothe.

"Tough night?" Nick the cabbie asked.

I shrugged. "Regular. Just more tired than usual."

He nodded and started the car. I looked out the window as we cruised to my small building. It wasn't in a particularly good part of town, but then again most of the town wasn't a good part. Not by most people's standards. By mine it was a hell of a lot better than what I'd grown up in. My parents used to rent a beat-up, one-bedroom apartment in a smaller city than this, in a worse part of town than mine was, for sure. My current bedroom was as big as our family room from back there, and the plumbing was much, much better where I was now. Maybe my life wasn't the best, or even that good. But I knew for a fact it could be a hell of a lot worse. Having a healthy perspective on things made a huge difference.

I looked back at Nick's regular raggedy hat and fought off reminiscing. It was a toxic sport for me.

"How are the kids?"

He smiled in the rearview mirror. "Little one had a ballet recital today."

I loved the way his voice smiled when he talked about his family. Nick was as close to a bearable father figure as I'd seen in a while. He was kind and loved his kids, maybe even his wife. It restored my dwindling faith in the human race to hear him talk about them.

"Did she do well?"

"I don't know squat about ballet, but she did great."

"How would you know if you don't know squat about it?"

He chuckled. "She's my kid. She always does great."

I smiled and fiddled with my bag. "Keep that in mind for when she reaches puberty."

He laughed and took my money just as the dark shape of my building came into view.

"Bye, Nick."

He waved me off and waited for me to go inside before driving away. Nick had been my ride home every night I'd worked for almost a year. He'd showed up for a couple of calls in the beginning, and then we just settled on him swinging by every time I needed that ride home. I'd call; he'd be there. He could use the money, and I could use the relief of knowing who drove me home.

My building was old and it smelled a bit funny. Not actually bad, but funny enough to make you wonder just what the smell was. It was a one-story sort of deal, and I had to climb up a dozen or so stairs to get to the hall and my door. It wasn't a big hall, and at each end of it was one apartment door. One was mine, the other Doug's, my sexy neighbor. He was part of the night people tribe, just as I was. Though he was more of the ass-kicking variety, a bouncer. My keys clicked and echoed through the small hall as I unlocked.

"You haven't been answering my calls."

I froze as a voice I knew quite well drifted through me. At this point the door was already open. He could come in if he so much as pushed against me. Somewhere in the mess of my bag was a phone, but who would I call? Tony? It would take him too long to get here. Was Doug working tonight? I inhaled deeply and turned to face Richie.

"What are you doing here?"

He pushed off the wall and came out of the darkness. The place wasn't lit up but a window threw enough light from outside that I could make out his face. He had that creepy grin on, the one that advertised he was trouble. I used to love that grin back when I didn't know it was a real warning.

"If the queen won't come to her king…"

He trailed off as his eyes ran over my body. I felt naked though I wasn't.

"I'm not the queen to your king, Richie. Not anymore."

"Sure you are, baby," he cooed. "Aren't you inviting me in?"

"Go home. You're drunk."

It was a gross understatement. He stank to high heaven of booze. Only came around when he was drunk. He was also prone to violence when he was drunk—I knew from personal experience. My heart began to pound like crazy as he staggered closer.

"Hey, you heard the lady. Beat it."

I slumped against the door as Doug came out of his apartment. Richie wasn't a small man by any standards; he was tall and well built but not fighting-fit. Doug, on the other hand, was a well-known ass-kicker and packed a damn heavy punch. Richie gave him the age-old once-over, did the math on it, and decided he'd get his ass whooped. He turned tail and shuffled away, leaning against the walls.

Doug walked up to me and leaned his shoulder against the wall by the door.

"You sure do know how to pick 'em, Bea."

I sighed. "Tell me about it. Want a beer or something?"

"Sure."

We walked in and I locked the door, just in case lover-boy decided to come back. Richie stalking around was enough of a reason to move, but I couldn't afford it yet. Besides, I liked having Doug next door. New neighbors wouldn't look out for me like he did, that was for sure. I didn't want to leave just because Richie got a severe case of the blues when he drank too much.

Doug fell on my couch and propped his feet up on the coffee table. "So, how's the job?"

Groan. "Sam wants me to get together a new costume. Again."

He frowned. "What's wrong with the one you have now?"

"No idea. I think he'd rather get a new dancer on my cube but Tony says he can't fire me, I've got those high-roller regulars. You know, like the Cristal guy. They asked for more of me, not less, so Sam can't give me the boot. And he's still pissed I turned down his stripping idea."

"Hmmm…maybe. What difference does a new costume make, then?"

I got his beer and one for me and slumped beside him on the couch. "Damned if I know. Maybe forcing me to splurge on costumes will get me broke and I'll give into stripping? Anyway, I have to come up with something, though I'm fresh out of ideas."

"I know this chick in a lingerie store. Maybe she can help you out."

"It can't be lingerie. That would've been easy."

"Yeah, but she knows more about that shit. Has a great collection of costumes in her personal wardrobe."

I laughed and punched his shoulder. "You dog!"

"Someone needs to show me some love if you won't," he said, pinching my shoulder.

I leaned my head back on the couch and stared at the ceiling. There were a few cracks there so I traced them with my gaze. Fresh ideas wouldn't hurt. I didn't really have any.

"Will you take me to meet this chick, then?"

"Yeah, sure. We can stop by her shop tomorrow."

I nodded. "Come over around eleven."

"It doesn't have to be the wee hours of the morning," he grumbled.

"That's close to middle of the day for normal people, Doug. It's only wee hours for us night people."

"Night people," he mused as he got up. "I like how that sounds. Fine, then. Eleven it'll be. See you tomorrow."

"Sleep tight," I called out after him.

"Make sure you lock up. That fucktard might be coming back later, and I'll seriously damage his ass if I lose sleep on his account."

I nodded and he walked out. That damaging of Richie's ass was something I might have wanted to watch from the peanut gallery. Doug was a monster of a man, tall and wide and built like a bulldozer. He kept his head shaved to show off the badass neck—as thick as his jaws—and the phoenix tattooed on his nape. The oranges and reds in it stood out against his dark chocolate skin. There had been a spark between us when I first moved in, but back then he had a girl. Then I hooked up with Richie, and by the time that was over, the spark between Doug and me had dwindled away. We'd become friends in the meantime. Now he was the sort of big-brother figure a girl had good reason to fantasize about on occasion.

I nursed my beer and took a swig now and then. My stomach grumbled for something more substantial, but I was just too tired to move. I turned on the TV and stared blankly at whatever commercial was on.

With no audience whatsoever, I had no energy to pull on to keep going. I tried to find some solace in the TV shows, a desperate measure that often backfired. This particular kick in the face came from a detergent commercial. The mom was doing dishes in the sink, looking all haggard and exhausted. Then the dad and kid galloped in with this new dish cleaner that would do so much better than any other. The last images were of them hugging and kissing and the mountains of clean dishes gleaming in the background. If he really loved her, he'd get a damn dishwasher— that was my take. But that happy family picture kicked where it hurt the most. For a horrible moment I saw my parents and myself in there, hugging and kissing like the perfect little family. My stomach lurched into my throat and eardrums began to ring.

Tears rushed down my cheeks, and I didn't bother to swipe them away. Make-up melted and ran down my cheeks. I was a clown with a runny face. The now-empty beer bottle clanked against the floor. It didn't break, just rolled to hide somewhere, camouflaging its emptiness under the pretty tag. Tossed away after being drained, a useless, good-looking thing nobody cared about that had nothing more to give. At least if it had broken, the shards would have gotten someone's attention.

Maybe breaking was better.

Chapter 2

I woke up to banging on the door. Before long, the banging was accompanied by the annoying semi-shouting of Doug.

"You better get your ass up and open this door, Bea."

I shook my head and auto-piloted up to open. My face felt cakey, and a nasty headache crawled behind my eyes. Doug stood there, hands digging deep in his pockets.

"You coming in or what?" I mumbled.

His eyes looked sort of sad, way too sad for the morning hour. I turned around, scratching my nape. My hair was a mess and I realized my face must be worse.

"Come on, get in. Quick shower and I'll be good in no time."

"I highly doubt that," he said as he closed the door behind him. "Did that fucktard come back or call or something?"

"Who, Richie? Nah. I drank too much beer and crashed on the couch."

I got in the bathroom and closed the door, leaned against it for a while. My head still felt heavy, thoughts crawling sluggishly through my mind. Mornings sucked. Having a friend tell you looked like crap didn't help matters, either. That was totally not the way to start the day.

As soon as I faced the mirror, I winced. The sight was worse than a warmed-over zombie. Poor Doug, having to see that in the morning. I scrubbed my face clean, took a quick shower, and washed my hair. Some make-up covered the dark circles under my eyes and brought back the false glow to my face. I tied the bathrobe around me and got out.

Doug slumped in the couch, flipping through channels.

"Much better presentation," he said, smiling.

I rolled my eyes and walked into the bedroom. "Wait till you see me all dressed up. So, is this chick we're going to see your ex or what? Having some ex who owns a lingerie store would be totally hot," I called through the closed door.

"She's a fucking fantasy, more like."

Snort. "How romantic. You're all heart, huh?"

I came out with my shades tucked on my head, wearing jeans and a shirt. Wallet and phone were stuffed in my pockets, and I rolled the house keys around my finger.

"I am all heart, Bea," he murmured from a step away.

I looked up into smoldering black eyes. It always had me short on air when I got hit by the force of his eyes in the morning light. There was something there, something hungry and consuming. It scared me. I took a step back and gulped.

"Relax, doll. Much too early for me to hit on anyone," he said, smiling.

The scorching intensity evaporated. Playful Doug was back, the slick grin and casual manner restored. I smiled up, trying to say my "thank you" without words. He seemed to get it, but that look remained in the back of my mind. I'd thought that spark had dwindled away. Guess I was wrong. "So are we going or what?"

He grinned. "On one condition. I get to see you try on any costume contenders."

"Pfffft. In your dreams, big guy."

He *tsked* me and twitched his head toward the door. "Come on, then, haven't got all day."

His SUV was parked right by the entrance. Cars said a lot about men, just like shoes said a lot about women. The massive, dark purple SUV suited Doug to a T: brazen, in your face, strong, and seductive. I wondered if the size of the car-size of the ding-dong thing applied and just how small a dong a guy had to have to go for a monster car. It was probably mean to think so; he could have been imagining what those flats I wore said about me based on the same stereotypes. I looked down at my cherry-red shoes and wondered if I fit the picture. A guy like him should walk around with one of those ridiculously perfect women, boobalicious model-like felines that purred at you with every stare. I was probably bringing his brand down this morning.

"Is this place far? Can't we walk there, maybe?"

He stared at me like I was insane.

"So first you had me get up at goddamn eleven in the morning, now you want to walk there? Are you exploring your sadistic streak these days?"

I scrunched my nose at him, putting on my best fifth-grade teacher face on as I pointed a finger. "Walking won't kill you."

"The hell it won't. This place is across town. I like you fine, but I don't like you *that* much. Get your ass in the car, and next time you have a bright idea like that, shut up about it."

I snorted but did as told. It wasn't wise to mess with big-ass men in the morning. They were like Godzilla after a year of dieting: ready to bite your head off. He kept mumbling about my bright ideas for a while as he drove. I tried to turn on some music but he turned the volume down and clacked his lips.

"I get enough of that shit at work. Lemme enjoy some peace and quiet, doll."

"Aside from your grumbling, you mean," I added innocently.

He shook his head. "I'm regretting this trip already."

His grumpy act was part of why I liked hanging out with him so much. He had a way of frothing at the mouth that made me laugh, and I could always tell by his eyes when he was only acting grumpy to come off as more of a tough guy. Doug was a closet gentleman and all-around sweet guy. He probably thought it didn't suit the jaw-smasher vibe his general appearance came with, so always did the frowning and growling thing to look all fierce. As far as I was concerned, he was just an oversized teddy bear.

I knew immediately when we reached the shop in question. Its smoking hot sexiness vibe radiated a block wide. The shop window was dark tinted, some subtle magenta glow putting the display mannequin in the kind of dark and luscious light that made you want to sway your hips more when you walked.

I watched Doug out the corner of my eye as he walked up to the door. He opened the thing and nodded at me to get a move on. Growling, but still a gentleman to his ever-blooming shame. The man seemed crankier than me in the morning, and I hadn't even had coffee yet. It was the dark nectar of the gods that brought me fully into civil human-being mode. Between Doug and me, I ventured a guess I'd have the worse bite right about now.

Once we were inside, I got shivers up my spine. Chains, leather, corsets, and insane fuck-me heels hung from every part of the place. Magenta walls lit by soft lights, black-and-white pictures of people wearing ropes, cuffs, collars. Goddamn, my skin prickled up.

"Is there something you'd like to tell me, Doug?" I whispered.

He poked me in the ribs as the most gorgeous woman I'd ever seen walked over to us. The way she moved was hypnotizing. She had long, lean legs. Her feet were clad in high heels sharp enough to poke your eyes out. She wore nothing overly provocative, but you wanted to lick her all over from one glance. Her light chocolate skin glowed almost gold, lush lips spread in a soft, almost indulgent smile. I blinked a few times, had to shake my head. And I wasn't into women.

"Sweet Mary, mother of my ever-loving God," I whispered.

Doug cleared his throat. "Hey, Justine."

No freaking way she was called Justine, too. Was the Marquis de Sade going to jump out from around a corner and wink? I crossed my arms over my chest.

"Douglas. Always a pleasure to see you in the shop. And who's your lovely friend?"

Perfect. I was too busy ogling her up to introduce myself. I shook my head. "Sorry, I'm Bea. Nice to meet you."

She reached out a perfectly manicured hand and shook mine. "And Bea is short for…?" she asked smiling.

I was blinded. "Beatrice."

"Ah, much better. Beatrice, what can I do for you?"

Doug cleared his throat again. "We were wondering if you'd help her put together a new costume. She's a dancer over at Sam's Pearl on Hans street."

She gave me a slow once over. "Really? Why would a lovely girl like you work in such a dump? I sincerely hope it has nothing to do with a personal relationship with Sam."

I chuckled. "No worries there. We hate each other, but that's not much of a relationship, I guess. Tony's all right though."

She shrugged but her smile warmed a bit. "So you're one of the stubborn ones, then."

I scrunched my eyebrows. She cocked her head to the side. "I'm guessing he suggested a…career adjustment and you said no. Is this your first costume change?"

I huffed out a breath. "My sixth in the last eight or so months."

Her beautifully arched eyebrows went up. It looked funny. "You must be very good to last that long."

"I guess. But I'm going to get fired soon anyway, huh?"

She nodded. "So you'd like to put together a new costume? Have any pics of your previous ones?"

I took out my phone and showed her a few. She had a special way of focusing on things, I noticed. It felt more intense, like she was giving the object of her attention a special kind of care, something beyond the norm. It was the same kind of attention Doug gave her when she wasn't looking. Whatever spark had been or was between us, the man had it *really* bad for Justine. Couldn't blame him, really. The woman was breathing artwork.

"Have you considered a change in style?" she asked after studying my pics.

I shrugged in an, "oh, what the hell" way. "What do you have in mind?"

"First I'd need to see you dance. You know everyone has their own flavor. I think we need to match your dance with your costume. It will help cement the attention of your admirers if you manage to find just the right vibe."

I loved her immediately. "So, do I just dance here, or…?"

She held up one finger. Heels clicked sharply against the floor as she walked over to the small counter. Music crawled out of the woodwork. There were no speakers or anything of the sort that I could see, and yet the sound clarity was beautiful. I felt the familiar rush crawl up from the soles of my feet to the top of my head. Surprisingly it was a song I liked, a sensuous beat I wanted to dance to.

"Can I get some props from around here?" I dared ask.

She nodded and zoned in on me as I walked slowly around the shop. Crimson high heels, a small black hat tilted to hide my eyes. The jeans were tight enough to show my every move, so I just needed one more element. A glossy red cane with a head shaped like a rose screamed to be picked up. I ran my hands over it, tested its height. With those heels it suited me perfectly.

By the time I was done getting my gear ready, the song changed. The beat called to me as it flowed around the shop. I smiled and began to sway my hips with each step as I walked back closer to them. When I found a post I liked, I poked the ground with the glossy red cane. Circling around that point, I visualized my fans. It always helped me put more heart into it. My body began to flow with the music—slow, sensuous moves and sways coupled with brusque twists and turns, slow steps in this or that direction. Now and then I threw them a look from beneath my titled hat, just to make sure I still had their full attention.

I moved my hips in wide circles, as my ankles remained glued to one another. The support of the cane helped me put in moves I only longed to accomplish without one. I snaked to kneel on the floor, grabbed the cane with my hands as it stood at the small of my back. My pose was slightly reminiscent of tied-up hands, probably because of the décor. My upper body writhed as if I were a captive. My pulse rushed and I slowly got up and turned around, facing away from them. I crossed my legs at the ankles and leaned forward, putting my whole weight on the cane I held in front of me.

As if rehearsed, the song changed. Tanya Stephens's "Can't Breathe" slithered through my bones next. I parted my legs, still holding my weight on the cane. Bones became loose, liquid. I allowed the music to take me over completely, lost in the delicious torture of the lyrics. The mood of the song gripped my stomach tight, and I relished the despair that echoed through my skin.

Yes, this was what I lived for. My salvation. This gave me wings. Speaking through every motion of my body, pulling and pushing every part of me to scream what the song whispered inside my heart. Sweat began to glide down the middle of my spine and between my breasts. I fell one level deeper inside, relished the toxic need that crawled out. Moderately aware of what I was doing, I saw my body move as in a mirror. I marveled at the lush movements, admired the abandon on the face half hiding under the hat.

The music stopped abruptly. My heart was pounding furiously. I generally danced with less enthusiasm over at Sam's club, but then again they only played house at the Pearl. This richer, deeper kind of music called to me. It summoned movement out my body, bypassing my mind entirely. I licked my lips and looked up, awakened from the dancing high.

Justine stared at me in a different way, assessing but hot at the same time. It made me suck in a breath, that kind of impossible focus squeezing my insides. Beside her, Doug shook his head and rearranged his pants.

"Hot damn, Bea. I'm coming to see you dance every night from now on, even if it gets me fired."

He sounded gruff, turned on like hell. I grinned at him and relished the power. It was what had my fans coming back, night after night—that craving. But Justine's reaction was different. Her interest was more engaged than his, though it offered me no power at all. If anything, it took it away from me. The chemistry of that reaction had my skin prickling up, my legs twitching to step back.

"Whatever Sam pays you, I'll pay you three times that to dance in our club."

Her eyes sparkled with determination and she slithered close, one step at a time. Each step she took made my spine tingle with something strange, a new sort of power vibe washing through me. I wasn't thriving on it as much as she was, though. She was doing the taking this time, not me. And whatever that chemistry woke inside me, she responded to it naturally. She was another breed from what I'd known or felt until then. That vibe, that chemistry had my tummy tingling.

I cleared my throat and smiled, cool as I could be. "You don't even know how much he pays me."

"I want you in my club," she said, smiling with confidence.

I felt it in my bones that she knew she had me. I hadn't agreed to anything, but she knew she had me. Her expression turned triumphant, and she hooked her arm around mine.

"Now let's get you the right costume, Beatrice."

"Just to be clear, I don't strip. Or anything but dance," I added in a rush.

She chuckled. "No fear. I only want you to dance. You can trust Doug to keep you safe in case anything happens."

I frowned. "I thought Doug worked in a kinky club of sorts."

She grinned. "Yes, ours. But it's not as kinky as you think. Well, at least the part you'll be dancing in isn't."

I stopped dead in my tracks. "I'm not agreeing to anything until I see the place in full swing."

"I like smart girls. Let's pick your costume now, and you stop by tonight. Check the place out. See how you feel about it. If it makes you want to dance, then you can start tonight. If not, we part ways friends, and the costume will be my gift to you with my best wishes for the future. Sounds good?"

She didn't strike me as a woman who didn't get her way, but the deal sounded solid. At the worst, I'd get a free costume out of it. All I had to do was go out to this other place on my free night from the Pearl, check things out. Sounded like a good deal. Doug leaned against that counter as we flittered around the shop. She had all sorts of things in there, a lot centered around leather and metal, some latex and feathers even. I had a good idea what kind of club hers would be.

After we got my costume together, I got pink cheeks staring at it in the mirror. She assessed me with a professional eye, and her face glowed with a job well done.

"You'll kill tonight with that outfit," she whispered, satisfied.

"If I decide to stay," I added. "You haven't asked me how much I make at the Pearl. What if you decide you don't want me?"

Her eyes found mine in the mirror and held them. "Whatever it is, you're worth it. And I've already decided I want you. You're exactly what Satine needs."

I breathed in deep and looked at myself in the mirror again. The costume looked hot as all hell, I had to give her that. The idea of dancing in that kind of outfit had my blood pumping. "So what kind of music will I dance to?"

She shrugged. "Your choice entirely. Dancing is art. I wouldn't dream to tell artists what to do, now would I? You work it out with the DJ at the Satine. But the man is very good at reading people, so I think he'll give you exactly what you want on instinct."

That totally sounded kinky. I blinked hard a couple of times. Sam's view on it was we wiggled to whatever music was on to keep customers pouring in. Justine was giving me the kind of respect I had for performers of all kinds. She saw art in my dancing, gave me creative freedom with it? It sounded like too good a deal.

With my bags in tow, Doug and I said goodbye to Justine and got back to his car.

"You didn't have anything to do with this, did you?" I asked, narrowing my eyes.

He shrugged. "She knows style and shit. I was sure she could help you out with the costume thing. I had no idea if she'd want to offer you a job along with it. I hoped, I admit."

"Why?"

"I work there. I know the place. And I know that shit Sam, too. Justine's a real lady—she wouldn't push for anything you don't want to do. You'd be much better off working for her."

I studied my hands in my lap. He was probably right; he'd worked for basically everyone in town so he did know his stuff. But Justine's place had a headier flavor to it; I could tell from the costume we'd picked up. Changing environments wasn't a good idea for me, by and large. New places meant new possibilities of freak-outs. "And you'd be there if anything goes wacky."

"Yeah. I'd also be your ride. That fucktard Richie would get the message loud and clear and stay away."

"He only shows up when he's drunk," I grumbled.

"Which is getting to be a not-so-rare event."

I knew he was right, but something rubbed me the wrong way about the whole situation. Maybe him trying to go too Daddy on me. Wasn't something I reacted to well, but at least I didn't freak out with Doug. I trusted him—probably a foolish risk to take. But one I'd already taken a while back. He respected my limits overall, didn't think I was too big of a freak, and never asked. I liked him, but we weren't going to discuss my ex. One more thing to put on the list of "never to go there."

"So there are other dancers at the Satine?"

"Yeah, a couple. The area you'd dance in is a new addition. The place keeps expanding. Business is good for Justine and Gowl."

My head snapped up. "Justine and who?"

"Gowl, her business partner. Chill, it's not Pearl's version of Tony if that's what you're thinking. He's not that hands-on, really. Technically the shop and the Playroom are Justine's area, and Gowl deals with the lounge and Satine."

"She just gave me a job without asking him?"

He shrugged. "He's not too keen on details, I guess. I dunno, doll. Maybe he'll interview you tonight if you decide you want the job."

"Right. How can you not know about your other boss?"

"Believe me, Justine is more than enough to worry about."

I frowned and poked his arm. "What's that supposed to mean? Didn't you say she was your squeeze?"

His hands gripped the wheel harder, eyes straight ahead on the road. "No, I didn't. You just jumped to that conclusion."

"There's something weird about this whole thing. What are you not telling me?"

He shrugged. "You'll see tonight and decide for yourself."

Hmmm, mysterious answer. I grinned. "Will you be wearing leather pants and studs on your ding-dong?"

He snorted. "Ding-dong? What are you, seven? No, I wear a suit."

"But other people wear leather and metal on their—"

He cut me off, holding a hand up.

"You'll just see tonight, all right? Be ready for about eight. We're leaving at eight thirty the latest. My shift starts at nine, but I like to get there a bit early."

"And ogle Justine in all her brilliant glory?" I added innocently.

He shook his head. "I'm so regretting this already."

Chapter 3

I spent about two hours putting together my outfit. The costume was safely tucked in my big bag, and I'd taken the crimson shoes out and walked around the house with them all day. If I were going to dance in them, they'd need some getting used to. They had a good grip on my ankles and felt sturdy enough, though they looked like naughty fuck-me heels. I'd never danced in something that cheeky, but I loved the way they looked. So I'd wear them tonight, dancing or no dancing. They were a gift, anyway, weren't they?

I decided to do some black, form-fitting pants and a low-cut, black blouse with generous enough cleavage to make you look but not enough to make you stare. My hair was puffed up in a loose bun, bangs hanging over my eyes. The red highlights stood out against my bangs and the rest of my black hair. I loved black and red—probably why my dancing costume ended up in that combination. I went with some bangles on my arm and big hoops for my ears. Went to town a bit with the black around my eyes and pale pink lip-gloss. The dark makeup made my eyes stand out like crazy. They were my favorite things about my looks, a honey color almost light enough to be yellow.

My mom had eyes like that. Each time I looked in the mirror, I thought of her. And every time I did, I thought of my father and that horrible day two years ago. It cut my air and made my head spin, so I quickly turned on some loud music and began to dance around the living room. Nothing major, just letting music displace my thoughts. I carried around an mp3 player in my bag for those times I really needed a music intervention. Music had always been my escape. After I lost my parents it didn't occur to me to do anything else but pursue music down any paths it would take me. I didn't have the vocals, but I had the moves. College wasn't even close to an option. My family had been piss-poor when my parents were alive, and by myself I wasn't doing any better.

I suddenly stopped dancing around when I realized Doug was standing there, arms crossed over his chest.

"You realize I've been here for like five minutes?"

"Barge in on me, why don't you?" I said, narrowing my eyes.

"Your goddamn door was open. Do you care about your safety at all?"

Oops. I bit my lip and fluttered mascara-filled lashes at him. "Sorry. Got all carried away with getting ready for tonight."

He looked mildly appeased. "My shift starts earlier. The guy on call before me had to leave. You ready to go?"

I nodded and grabbed my bag. Phone, wallet, keys, dancing costume of obscene sexiness—a girl could take over the world with just that. Or at least I hoped so.

The drive there seemed very familiar. "Is this place close to Justine's shop?"

He nodded, attention set on the parking-spot hunt. *Men.* Everything had to be a project. "It's right at the back and under. Let me just find a spot, and I'll give you a tour."

I sighed and let him do his thing. The shop was now closed, but I noticed *the Leather & Chains* sign upfront. Hadn't noticed that earlier. I couldn't have described the place better than that sign, I had to admit. If they stuck up a picture of Justine, customers would probably assault the place with abandon. Behind the shop stood a building a bit taller and pretty wide. Was that the club? Doug finally parked and we hopped out of the SUV.

"Main entrance is on the other side, but we can go through the alley entrance."

"We're with the in crowd, huh?" I asked, all giddy.

He smiled and pressed a hand to the middle of my back as we went in. The door screeched ominously when it closed behind us. It was fairly dark, and some stairs sloped down before us. Orange light came from the lower level.

He went down two stairs at a time, leaving me to rush behind. I hated it when they did that. Weren't the heels obvious enough? Did those things look like a girl could gallop in them?

"Come on, Doug! I'm wearing fuck-me heels. Stop running around like a squirrel on speed, will you?"

I bumped into a wall, of course. Just my luck, the entrance of doofuses worldwide: bumping into stuff. Generally very publicly, too, or there'd be no point in making a fool of yourself. Awkward and crowds went together like milk and cookies. I massaged my nose and took a step back to assess the situation. Maybe I'd be spared some humiliation if I didn't have that big of an audience. That's when I realized it wasn't really a wall but a guy.

"Excuse you," I muttered, still holding my nose.

"For?" he asked seriously.

I frowned. "I'm sorry?"

"Apology accepted. Do look where you're going next time. It would be a pity to ruin that cute little button nose of yours."

His grin was highly annoying. I narrowed my eyes. "I'm not apologizing because you have the weird fetish of playing wall to a girl's face as she climbs down the stairs in f…ughhh, heels."

"Fuck-you heels, to be more exact," he said staring down at them.

My face heated up. "Ugh…"

"And I so would love to," he said.

"What's that supposed to mean? You would love to what?"

"I would so love to fuck you. But playing wall to your nose isn't one of my fetishes. I could give you a list of the ones I do have, though. Forget the list—let's do a crash course."

My mouth flapped open and closed a few times. My eyes were wide, and I could see how amusing he found it; that bastard smirk on his face grew from deviant to full-fledged evil mastermind. It only annoyed me more since it made my tummy tingle.

"Anthony, don't harass the girl. She'll never work for us if you scare her off the first day."

I stepped aside the offending man-wall to see Justine standing there. She wore leather tights, a corset that puffed her boobs up to her chin, and sported some very hot fuck-me, knee-high boots. I did a double take.

"Wow." It was out of my lips before I could stop it. Man-wall frowned and stepped in front of me, searching my gaze.

"I really hope you don't swing that way."

I snorted. "Which way should I swing?"

"Mine," he said with a casual smile.

"Only thing I'm likely to swing your way is a bat," I answered, smiling congenially.

Behind him, Justine burst out laughing. She had the kind of laugh that made you feel not sophisticated enough. Was the woman perfect? I looked down at my shoes again.

A big, rough paw came into my line of sight and one of the fingers on said paw pushed my chin up. The dark eyes of man-wall met mine and held my gaze in a way old friends should, not perfect strangers.

"I would love to," he whispered again. "Each time I look at those shoes, I think I'd very much love to fuck you. And now you'll think of that each time you see them, too."

With that, the bastard just turned around and walked away. I blinked a couple of times at his back until he turned around a corner and disappeared from sight. I was flabbergasted.

"He tends to have that effect on people," Justine said with a strange air of pride.

I ignored her blatant beauty and frowned. "Is it technically too early to sue for sexual harassment if I'm not under contract with you? Because I would go the extra mile for this guy."

She chuckled and waved my comment off as if it were a fly. "I haven't seen him be that rude to anyone since we were in third grade."

Was she unfortunate enough to have known him for that long? The woman was in need of some serious commiserations.

"Obviously he hasn't come a long way since then," I muttered under my breath.

Her eyes sparkled. These were weird people. "I think having you here will prove to be even better entertainment than I'd hoped. That, by the way, was Anthony. He's not generally concerned with the details of our business. In fact, he rarely comes out of his office these days."

I would have pegged him for a control freak with obsessive attention to detail, really. Chilled out and not poking around for details about a place he ran didn't fit the picture. Overbearing asshole was more like the general feel I'd gotten.

"Just my luck he did come out tonight, huh?"

"Positively better entertainment than I'd hoped," she said with twisted satisfaction. "Let me give you a tour. Douglas had to go cover security."

Clearly Justine had a fetish for using whole names. Along with others, surely, by the looks of things. Somehow her beauty was less arresting in this gear than it had been today in the shop. At least now she looked like she wanted to get your attention, so you didn't feel weirded out by how easily she got it. In the shop, though, when she'd worn nothing overly attention seeking, it had unnerved me to realize how easily she became anyone's focus point. I wondered what kind of personality she must have to put up with that annoying man-wall. She was either a saint or just as bad as him, and I couldn't decide right then which would likely annoy me more.

The place was beautiful. It smelled like dark chocolate and woods at night, when everything is chilly as it touches your face. Walking through the place was like entering a different world. Heavy drapes hung everywhere, deep burgundies and candle-looking lamps all over the place. Very gothic but not overdone.

The first area we entered was a lounge and restaurant area with private booths. Each booth had a set of heavy, burgundy drapes hanging at its entrance. A couple of them were already pulled shut, and I couldn't help but wonder what could be going on inside. Did they encourage playing around in here? The place had a deeply sensual vibe, and it just got you into a frisky state of mind. We went through a narrow hall on the left that led to a set of closed, heavy doors.

"This is the Playroom area," Justine said, following my gaze.

I frowned. "Playroom area?"

I could bet it wasn't rummy they played back there. The heavy doors slipped open just a bit. Music glided out from behind the open doors, and just then a desperate scream echoed through the hall we were in. My eyes widened, and I stared dumbstruck at Justine.

"I think it's clear the sort of play, hm?" she said, grinning.

She gave me chills right then. I wanted to step back, maybe even turn tail and get the hell out of there. I had no issues with sensuality, but what seemed like pain freaked the hell out of me. That scream sounded like pain to my ears, and lots of it.

"Relax," a deep voice said from behind me.

I jumped and found they had me surrounded. The panic subsided a bit as I realized Doug was here somewhere. Though these people seemed to be able to do real damage very quickly, so I wasn't sure how much comfort Doug's hypothetical presence really brought me.

Wall-man walked with his hands in his pockets, eyes still playful but his face serious. "She's about ready to use those pretty fuck-her heels in a sprint if you keep it up, Tina."

Her eyes narrowed, but they didn't flash aggression as much as brotherly annoyance. "You think you can handle the tour better? Be my guest. I'll see you later if he screws it up, Beatrice. Let me know how lousy he was at it."

With that she just turned on her high heels and clicked away. Holly hell, was everyone insane down here? Obviously dramatic exits were part of the job description.

"Whenever she goes overboard, just call her Tina. She'll run for the hills, as you can see."

He made me laugh, though I resented him for it. I cocked my head to the side and gave him my sternest glare. "Yeah, but that leaves me with you and no idea how to get you running for the hills if you go overboard."

He grinned and leaned back against the wall. "That's easy. You can't. So, let's get this tour over with. Then we can talk."

He pushed off the wall and began walking without a look back. He just assumed I'd walk behind him, of course. Which made him an ass and a big one. I didn't deal well with asses, though he did have a very cute one, I had to admit. I shook my head and focused on his shoulders. He was nice and tall, wide in the shoulders and pretty narrow in the hips. A big man, and I liked those. Why was I checking him out, again? The guy was an ass, regardless of how cute his actual ass was.

There was some ambient music playing in the hall and restaurant area, but nothing too loud like in the Playroom area. I shuddered, remembering that particular part, though it had been obvious what kind of club they ran from the shop upstairs. Still,

I got the chills. Some of my worst fears were someone's pleasures here, and that thought kept buzzing right behind my eyes.

Wall-man stopped walking without warning so I again ended up splatting face-first into him, this time into his back. He sighed and turned around. "I'm starting to think you actually like me but don't know how to convey the message. A smile would be enough, you know—no need to throw yourself into me like this at every opportunity."

My arm went up, maybe to slap him, I had no idea. None of us would find out, because his hand was lightning-quick to grab mine. His thumb rubbed against the inner side of my wrist, and he looked at the way it fit into his monster-paw with something akin fascination. Electrical shocks danced between us at the point of contact.

"That, I really wouldn't advise," he said calmly.

His eyes returned to mine. My throat got dry.

"Well, stop acting like a monster-sized ass, and then I won't get the urge to!" I snapped.

"This idea of your urges, it intrigues me."

My left eye began to twitch. "You're gonna give me a tic if you keep it up," I almost growled.

"Hmmm...I do tend to keep it up a long time. Never got complaints. Well, not the real kind."

This guy was just too much. I stared at him in open disbelief. "You're kidding me, right? You did not just say..."

He let go of my hand and pushed open a door. Some dark, luscious music attacked me from the room inside. It was a tall, dark place, packed with people. He grabbed my arm again and pushed through the crowd. Many of the unsuspecting push-by victims turned to give him more room as he bulldozed his way around. I briefly entertained the idea of tripping him, but we'd both fall down and kill my joy.

When we were near the middle of the room, he suddenly turned around. Yes, I did bump into his chest again. This time he'd done it on purpose to get me there, though. He grinned down and kept me there, bump in close. I squinted my eyes and tried to stick one of my heels into his foot, but he caught on and moved his foot away. The bastard. He leaned in and screamed into my ear so I could hear.

"Look up. That's working spot number one."

"Are you insane…" but I trailed off as I saw the cages.

Birdcage looking, but big enough for a person—three of them hung from the ceiling. Actually hung from the ceiling by chains. I got the chills and tried to step back. He held on, though, kept me rooted in place right against him.

"Relax," he said against my ear. "Those dancers might get violent if someone asks them to get out of their cages."

I looked at him like he was out of his mind, which I was pretty sure he was and opened my mouth to say as much. But he nodded into another direction and I followed his line of sight. In the far end of the room was a DJ booth and, right in front of it, a cube about one yard lower than the actual booth.

"That's the spot we'd like you to perform in," he said, still keeping me in place.

I frowned and tried to push against him, but he wouldn't let go. "Excuse me, mind disengaging your body from mine?"

He shrugged as if he hadn't heard. I squinted my eyes and reached up to his ear. He didn't help any, didn't lean down, didn't turn his head to the side so I'd have easier access. I had to practically climb on top of him to get there. The bastard.

"Let go of me," I screamed in his ear.

He *tsked*, and somehow I heard that as clearly as if we were the only ones there. "I'm doing you a favor. This is a statement to everyone that you're off limits. I'm guessing you're not into getting grabbed."

I shivered. "Most certainly am not."

"Well," he said, brushing his lips against the shell of my ear, "then say 'thanks,' since I'm doing you a favor. If you're seen with me like this, it's gonna mean you're mine, all mine, and nobody will dare make a move on you."

"Gee, thanks."

I felt his lips grin against my ear. "My pleasure. Now that you know where you'd work, let's go talk about actually working here."

"But…"

Too late—we were moving again. He dragged me through the crowd as I clung to my bag. I realized my costume would fit brilliantly in here. After reaching the DJ booth area, I noticed a door right behind it. It said *Employees Only* in thick, bright red letters. He took us through it, and as soon as the door closed the music died down considerably. A short corridor was barely lit with orange light. He opened a door at the end of the corridor and light poured into the hall from whatever room was on the other side. Once we were finally inside I pulled my arm free and walked a couple of steps in front of him, casting my gaze around.

The place was at odds with the rest of the establishment. White walls, white hardwood floor, sparse and minimalist furniture all in black. It looked cold and impersonal, almost abrasive. "Your office, huh?"

He glanced over at my face. "Good guess. Sit down."

I looked around for a place to sit. That was when I noticed the large glass that provided a view of the dancing cube I'd be working on. Perfect. He could watch me dance. Just the image I needed to have floating around my mind—this creep ogling me. Another quick look around helped me spot his desk area with two chairs in front. I walked to one of them and sat down. He loomed right at the back of my chair for a few moments so I turned my head at him.

"Stiff legs or something? Why aren't you sitting down?"

He smiled. "Since you ask so nicely."

Damned man. He walked over and sat beside me.

"Something wrong with the chair at your desk? Or are you reluctant to deal with the boss position?" I asked as casually as I could.

"I deal *very* well with the boss position, trust me. Now, I'm assuming you brought a resume with you?"

"Uhm, well…not really. I mean, Justine—"

"You're trying to get a new job, and you came to the interview without a resume? Not a good sign as far as professionalism goes."

I resented the fatherly tone he took with me. I resented anything fatherly except hearing Nick, my cabby, talk about his kids.

"I was asked insistently to consider accepting this job. You got this wrong if you think I'm trying for it. You're trying to get me, not the other way around."

He leaned back in the chair and crossed his legs. "Am I that obvious?" he asked, grinning slyly.

"You're making me uncomfortable," I gritted out, staring at my knees.

"Why is that, Beatrice?"

"For one thing, you know my name though we haven't been introduced. And you didn't introduce yourself. If you'd like to talk about professionalism—"

"Fair point. Why else do I make you uncomfortable?"

"Would you let me finish at least once?" I exploded. He grinned wider. Goddamn man.

"I'd love to see you finish. But we were talking about why I make you uncomfortable."

I gritted my teeth and tightened my fist on the bag with the costume. No way in hell would I work here with this creep looming a few feet from me every night. "You're harassing me, for one thing."

"What else?"

"Does there have to be another reason?" I snapped, looking him in the eye.

"Finally," he murmured. "I'm Anthony Gowl, and I'm entirely fascinated to make your acquaintance. Now, as you've noticed, we run a niche club here, Beatrice. That means a lot of people will either be very Dommy or very subby. You need to deal with both, and honestly right now you don't seem able to handle that."

I took in the serious face and lack of pushiness and frowned. "You've been psyching me out?"

"The Playroom is a D/s oriented club. The rest of the place isn't, but most of our guests are. None of us here should project anything but the fact everyone of that community, or any other for that matter, is welcomed. You're not projecting that by freaking out when you hear someone's throes of passion."

"That was a scream. If that's the throes of passion—"

"See? Exactly what I mean. You're judgmental and intolerant."

I massaged one temple and inhaled deeply. "That's a very annoying habit you have, not letting people speak. Either you want to talk to me, in which case you shut up and listen while I speak, or you don't want to talk to me, in which case I'm getting out of here."

He smiled. "Sorry. It's just so fun to push your buttons. Can't seem to stop myself."

"I don't want to work here. I don't even know why I considered it. I have a good job at Sam's—"

"Not anymore."

I froze, listened to my heart beating for a while. He just sat there, all calm with his legs crossed and that smug, bastard face daring me to try to speak again. It took me a while to decide what I wanted to say.

"Would you mind not speaking in goddamn riddles? What do you mean, not anymore?"

He sighed and leaned forward. I naturally leaned back.

"Sam knows you're here now. This is your job, or you don't have one."

Chapter 4

"I must not have heard you right. Run that by me again."

"Tina is a…rare kind of person. When she gets her mind set on anything, she gets it."

"I'm not following."

"When you said you'd consider working here, you were as good as fired from the Pearl. I'd like to say I'm sorry, but sadly I must admit Tina has incredible instincts."

I blinked a few times. "Still not following."

"She…resolved the Pearl situation. You don't have a job there anymore. So unless you take this one, you have no job right now. That's the long and short of it."

"The long and short?"

Everything started spinning around me. I gripped the armrests of the chair, and for a moment black covered my field of vision. I thought I'd passed out. But I realized I was bent over, my forehead resting against the black chair. I gripped the costume bag so hard my fingers hurt, but no matter how much I wanted to let it go I couldn't.

"The long and short of it," I mumbled.

A pair of hands gripped me and got me up. I was okay until he tried to hold me. Until his arms closed around me and I felt like I couldn't breathe. I struggled wildly, managed to fall on my ass on the pristine floor. There was something deeply wrong about a person who had pristine white floors, I decided right then. He froze on the spot, and for the first time since we'd met he looked something other than smug. He looked worried, maybe even frazzled. He made to step closer but I held out my hand.

"Don't close in on me," I wheezed.

We stood there for a while, me panting and wheezing on the floor and him staring. How much more humiliating could it have gotten? Maybe if I'd peed on myself. So I tried to stay positive about it—there was still a way to go before that height. After a while he sat on the floor, level with me but a few feet away. That was good; it made my wheezing subside almost entirely.

"I don't know what to do to help you right now," he whispered softly. "Please, tell me what to do."

I shook my head, refused to meet his eyes. "It's just a…thing. It goes away if you just…don't close in on me."

He nodded. "Are you claustrophobic? Or—"

"No. I'm nothing. I mean, I have no medical issue."

"You just had a…an episode of some sort now. Clearly, there is *some* issue."

"Have a bit of the savior's complex there, Anthony?" I asked in a small voice. "Don't assume and presume things about me. I'm not a damsel in distress, I don't need or want your help, and if you ever—ever!—touch me again without my explicit consent, I will stab you in the eyes."

"What with?"

I looked at him like he was crazy. Because he clearly was. "What?" I asked incredulously.

"What will you stab me with? Will you carry a knife around specifically for that purpose? Or toothpicks? Will you carry those with you?"

I blinked. "You're insane."

He smiled, looking completely satisfied with himself. I burst out laughing, hysterical laughter, and he chuckled a bit. When my laughing fit ended, I sat there on the floor. Calm. No wheezing, no crisis, no need for music intervention. And I looked over at him, seeing him in a whole new light. He was this insane man who had made me laugh during a freak-out moment. And the freak-out had passed. As if to prove that point to us both, he got up, slowly walked to me, and reached out his hand. I studied it, the blunt power of his fingers, the sturdy joints. I looked up into his dark eyes, and the bottom of my stomach fell as he smiled.

"You must think I'm crazy, huh?" I mumbled.

He shook his head and kept his hand out, a silent call. I took my time, looked into his eyes, back at the hand, into his eyes again. But there was no wheezing, no freak-out. I inhaled deeply and allowed him to pull me to my feet. Once I was up, he held on, and for some insane reason I didn't try to get my hand back. Just left it there for him to worry about.

"I think you're heartbreakingly beautiful," he finally said. "Please give this place a chance. Give me a chance. Dance tonight, try it out. If it doesn't feel right, I promise I'll get you another job somewhere you'll want to work. I'll owe you that much because of what Tina did. Okay?"

I nodded and looked around for my bag. That costume was tucked in there, waiting to shine. So I decided I'd give the place a try. I was way too young to stop giving people chances, anyway. Also way too old to not make rent next month, and I didn't really trust his people skills at this point. Who'd do this guy a favor and hire me out of the blue?

Plus I was a jumper now. I'd jumped ship from one club to another. Nobody looked kindly on that. If you got fired, you got fired. But leaving one place for another made you dancer non grata, a little rat. I was a little rat now.

To be honest, I'd agreed to check the place out. So I might have decided to jump ship in the end, but what Justine had done went way too far. These people had no clue about what was and wasn't all right regarding someone's personal space. Did I want to deal with that? Not really. I especially wanted nothing to do with

Justine for a while. I could work the place for a month or two until I found another job. I might as well jump to my advantage now that I was a jumper, anyway.

I glanced out through the glass at, potentially, my new cube. It looked pretty standing there in front of the DJ booth. Satine was tall and wide and packed with people. The cages hung a ways away, more toward the middle of the room. I didn't get how someone could stay in those tiny prisons. It made me shiver to even look at them. Hell, it creeped me out to even think of them.

"Just to be clear, I won't work in one of those cages. And I won't go near the Playroom area. Not ever, are we clear?"

He walked over and stood beside me, hands in pockets. "It's liberating to dance in the cages, at least that's what the cage dancers say."

I shivered. "Being locked up in a cage with the bars closing in…That won't ever sound liberating. You can't make that make sense to me."

"If you have triggers, we need to cover that now."

I turned toward him and frowned. "Triggers?"

"Anything that takes you back to some sort of traumatic event. I'll do my best to make sure your immediate environment is free of triggers."

There he went, going all Daddy on me again. Getting me another job if I didn't take this one, now taking care of my environment. I wasn't even sure he realized how he was barging into my space. It was smooth, under cover of politeness, of course. It would have made me seem a bit odd to tell him to stick that care up where the sun didn't shine.

I had no idea what set me off, really. It could be just a simple touch from someone, or a space that was too tight. With Richie I never got a freak-out, not even if he was on top of me—and that was the worst kind of freak-out when I got it. It had been one of the reasons I'd been going out with him so long, and why I could easily fall back into it. Richie made me feel safe. Or at least he had, until that one night when he was drunk out of his mind. I shook my head.

"I'm fine. As long as nobody tries to play Daddy to me."

I winced at my own words, but it was most likely the best description. He looked, curiosity sparkling in those dark eyes. He was the daddy type. I could see it written all over his face.

"Care to expand on that?"

Not really. "Let's just say I have a very sensitive personal space. As long as no one tries to trample into it, everything should be fine. No touching, certainly no bossing around, no small enclosed spaces."

"Too bad. I was imagining you in some very touchy, bossing-around situations."

"That's not funny," I said, looking out at the cube. "Where will I change?"

"We have a changing room, but it's…a small enclosed space. Maybe you'd like to change in here?"

I shrugged. "This is a one-way window, right? I can see out but they can't see in?"

He nodded. "I'll wait outside, by the cube. Sound good?"

I nibbled on the inside of my cheek. "Yeah, all right."

After he got out, I took in a deep breath. The room felt so much bigger without him in it. He was a trigger waiting to happen at all times, or at least it seemed to me right then like he was. But he was willing to give me the job and find me another one if this didn't work out. Or at least he'd said so. I had no real reason to trust him. But he was my best chance right now, and that in itself was very sad.

I shimmied out of my clothes and into the costume Justine had helped me put together. The hat was a lifesaver—I could tilt it just so it would cover the cages. The corset was already done up from when Justine had put it on me earlier, so all I had to do was close each one of the clasps in front. It pushed my boobs up nicely and made my middle seem small even to me. My bottoms were the best part, more like boxers with rich ruffles covering the full length of them on all sides. They were the same kind of hot red the glossy cane was. Underneath the ruffly boxers, I put on some black fishnets. And the *piece de resistance*—elbow-high, black satin gloves. I left the bangles on my arms, riding high over the gloves, and fixed my bangs under the hat. To make sure it would serve my purpose, I tilted it to the side a bit and to the front. The hairpins went into their appropriate holes in the hat to keep it well secured to my head. It was a dancing outfit, after all.

I arranged my clothes neatly in the bag and left it on the chair I'd sat on. The thought of leaving my bra there in his office made me shudder for some reason. I licked my lips, stretched my arms and legs. Took a few steps around to loosen up my muscles. This was it. Showtime.

I came out from under the red *Employees Only* sign just as Florence and the Machine began to sing in the club. The DJ's booth was occupied by some guy, very goth looking and with kind eyes. He'd be my new best friend, music-man in the joint. Anthony was chatting him up when I came out, but he turned in the direction the DJ was looking, and even in the dark I just felt the way his eyes burned up when he saw me. I wasn't shy, but the slow way he looked up my legs, smiled at my ruffly red boxers, and the hunger that shone there as his glance slid up my corset, all the way up to my face…Yep, I definitely shivered.

His gaze stayed on me as I walked to my cube and climbed up the stairs at its back. This was it. I felt more eyes in the crowd fix on me. Another Florence and the Machine song started and I closed my eyes, gave my body over to it. My arms flew open, my upper body swinging to the side. The glossy red cane touched the ground, and everything about the place washed through my bones, fueled me up. A few more pairs of eyes fixed on me now, and I sucked in the energy. It revved up my blood. The beautiful tingle of music exploded through my body and my hips began to sway, my limbs to move. I spoke everything I felt right then, every muscle of my body straining to scream it all loud and clear. My head became light quickly, and the intoxicating beat kept up. The DJ changed bands or songs, but he kept that beautiful, luscious rhythm. I'd have to thank him later on; the music fit me perfectly. Everything was pounding through my system, pumping through my veins, and rushing through my heart.

I felt right up there, more so then I ever had in the Pearl. The vibe of the place was just a bit dark but so rich, so delicious. My gaze licked over the crowd now and then, satisfaction bubbling up stronger as more and more pairs of eyes fixed on me with that familiar hunger. The hunger I thrived on. A few of them came closer to the cube, but not too close. It was high enough you couldn't see me right if you were too close. I liked that even more than the vibe of the place.

I looked in the eyes of each of the ones watching me, smiled for them. Swayed a bit harder, gave that bit more. *I'm here for you. I know you're here for me right now.* The more you gave them, the more they gave back. That exchange was beautiful, intoxicating. The rush tingled all over my body, powered me up enough to never lose the spunkiness of every move. Dancing was a lot like making love; you fed on the enthusiasm and pleasure sparkling in your partner's eyes.

They said people danced like they made love, and I believed that. Because I danced like there was no tomorrow, gave my audience my all. I made love the same way, which was why Richie kept coming back to me like a drug addict. It was a need I understood—it was how I felt about dancing. But he and I were over, definitely. He'd closed that door on us both the night he got drunk enough to pull my hair and push me against the bed face down. My body shook as I remembered it, so I pushed the thought away and launched deeper into the song. This was my haven, my salvation, my joy. And I did my best to let everyone watching me know this was *it* for me.

Time flew by. Before long the crowd was thinning out and the music changed pace to something a bit slower. Going-home music, it was the hardest to dance to. It was a long-winded goodbye, the sadness of the imminent separation clamping up my muscles. The sadness of the impending end of night washed through me and settled back in the pit of my soul. I stood on my cube, bowed with utmost reverence, and turned to walk down. *See you tomorrow night*, I told the place, the walls, the floor, the beautiful feeling of being filled to the brim with energy—to all, *see you tomorrow night*. I'd be there, I knew that for sure.

Anthony stood at the end of the stairs of my cube. That hunger from earlier was still lodged in the back of his eyes. I knew that look. I knew what it meant as I climbed down the last step and looked up at him. My skin prickled all over as he smiled. Even though I had heels on, he was considerably taller. Admittedly, I wasn't that tall. Height was a big turn-on, though it should have scared me. Someone taller, wider could easily overpower you, and feeling overpowered scared the hell out of me. And yet it turned me on like nothing else. It'd been a couple of months since Richie and I had been together that way, and I missed it. Shivers traveled up my legs as Anthony's gaze intensified. I licked my lips, shook my head as to ask, "What?"

He smiled and nodded toward the door to his office. This was it. We'd go back there, and he'd let me know if the club and I would work out or not. I was hoping for a welcome, not a goodbye. I really loved the vibe of the place.

I walked up to the *Employees Only* sign and went through the doors, walked into his office, and stood there until he closed the door behind him. When he didn't show up in my field of vision, I turned around. He was leaning against the door, arms crossed over his chest and gaze so intense it made me step back a bit. The petrol-gray shirt bunched around his thick arms, black slacks looking crisp enough though it was end of the night. I loved men in suits. Yet another one of those frustrating contradictions I did my best to ignore. Right then he looked big, powerful, and hungry. And I responded to it too much for my liking.

"We're going to have a problem," he said darkly.

I blinked hard a couple of times. Sweat glided down my back and my legs. I had been dancing the hell out of myself for a couple of hours, after all. A sheen of wet hung on my chin and cheeks. I took the gloves off, walked over to my bag, and reached in to get some wet wipes. After I ran them over my face and patted my legs with the small towel I carried for that purpose, I looked back up.

"What's the problem?"

He sighed deeply and shook his head. "The room is gonna be too small for the massive crowds of groupies you'll attract."

I chuckled and moved my weight from one leg to another. Those heels weren't so great right now. They were more on the painful side. "Mind if we sit down for the rest of this discussion?"

He pushed away from the door and stalked closer to me.

"Don't," I said in a small voice.

But we both stared at my fuck-me heels, and they didn't move back. They also reminded me, and maybe him too, that he would very much like to—fuck me. It would be easy for me to fall into it, actually. After dancing I was at my weakest, blood still pumping strong and the desire to please still tingling in the back of my mind.

He breathed in deep and stepped closer, eating the space between us. "This is gonna be the second problem. I can't stay away. I wanted you since you bumped into me with that cute little nose of yours, but after watching you dance…"

His eyes turned to the glass and remained fixed on my cube. He inhaled deeply and looked back at me. "I'm going to have a stroke if you push me away."

"I have a boyfriend," I blurted out.

He smiled, more cruel than kind. "You're lying."

I stepped back, bumped into the damn chair. His hand shot out and gripped my elbow to help steady me.

"I'm not lying, and I'm not a cheater. So step back. Please."

That last word came out more as a croak, pretty much mortifying. I felt my face heat up. Why couldn't I have it easy for once? Just once, just this once. I liked the place. I wanted to dance here. I didn't want awkward entanglements with this guy, because he scared me almost as much as he made my spine tingle. If only things could be easy, just once.

"I can see why Tina was so determined to get you, Beatrice. And I'm letting you know, here and now, that I'm a *lot* more determined than that to get you."

Chapter 5

My heart struggled in my chest, stomach doing somersaults. "I'll sue for harassment if you keep this up."

He smiled and slowly reached out for my hand. He held it with great care, turned my palm up, and brought it to his lips. Shivers ran through me as he kissed my palm, then the pads of my fingers one at a time. Tenderness had the bad habit of dissolving my knees. His brand of tenderness got to me in a way nothing else had, and it scared me out of my mind. He was a different breed from anything I'd ever known before. Some sort of alien, invading parts of me I'd been keeping under tight lock and key for two years. Just like that, with a few kisses on the palm of my hand, he flipped my heart over, had it jumping between fear and horrible exhilaration.

"Wonderful. I'll have a list of attorneys who specialize in harassment lawsuits ready for you by tomorrow night. In the meantime…"

I tried to pull my hand away and winced when he wouldn't let go. We were only touching where his hand held mine, but it felt like he was groping me, pawing at me all over. It was intrusive because his eyes plunged right into my soul, because they stirred the monster of toxic waste there. I shivered all over. This had to stop.

"I'm asking you to please step back." I spoke as calmly as I could. "I'll start screaming if you don't."

He sighed. "Maybe no one will hear you. What will you do then?"

"Kick you. Maybe having your nuts scrambled by my heels will help you come back to your senses."

He chuckled and kissed my hand again, then stepped back. "You'll have to do better than that to fend off besotted admirers."

I snorted. "And besotted employers, obviously."

He walked over to his desk and sat down. Finally, some freaking distance between us.

"I have no intention of giving up. But don't worry. I won't push it too far."

"Like you did just a moment ago?"

He shrugged. "We all have our moments of weakness. I'm sorry if I offended you. I'm not used to women…"

I squinted. "Not throwing themselves at you?"

He chuckled. "You did throw yourself at me tonight, Beatrice. Three times, was it?"

"I bumped into you because you obviously have the amazing-man-wall fetish going on. That's an entirely different thing."

He leaned back in his chair, eyes inquisitive as he looked at me. "You're comfortable enough to talk to me now. Now that I'm a few feet away."

I swallowed thickly. Yes, my courage needed some free space to manifest. And he just loved to push that space and push me around. Definitely the daddy type. I should have thrown my shoe at his smug face—maybe that would get across the message I needed distance. But this guy, he was all about pushing. It was clear in those intoxicating dark eyes that this was a project for him now. Men and their projects, ugh!

"Let's make this clear, Mr. Gowl. I'm not interested in you in any way, shape, or form. I'm asking nicely that you stop pawing at me and behave like a normal human being would with his peers. Because you don't own me, and you're not going to. Are we clear?"

He pouted and shook his head. "Don't crush my dreams under your heels, darling."

I ignored him and began to rustle with my bag. "Please get out so I can change. It's been a long day, and I'd like to get home."

"In a minute. First, write down your full legal name here and your phone number so I can reach you. Don't look at me like that. I'll need to be able to reach you if you work here. I'll call for Doug in the meantime—I understand he's your ride home. Unless you'd like me to drive you?"

My face snapped up. "Not a chance. It would be very nice of you to call Doug, thanks."

I scribbled my name and number down and waited as he made the call.

"He'll be here in about ten minutes. I'll let you change. He'll be right outside."

"Thanks," I said crisply.

"Whatever I can do for you, it's my pleasure."

I thought of a couple different things he could do for me right then, and none of them would turn out to be that pleasant for him. But I shut up so he'd go. I was entirely too tired to keep chatting with his smug self. My shoulders already sagged in defeat, because this situation had disaster written all over it in huge, neon-red, capital letters.

When I was done changing, I got out and found Doug by the door. Mr. Gowl was nowhere in sight. Thank goodness for small miracles.

"Ready to go, doll?"

I nodded and followed him out. Once we got into his car, he turned toward me. "I'm sorry. I found out what Justine did, I had no idea she'd be that—"

"Bitchy? Conniving?" I filled in bitterly. "As her schmuck partner put it, either I have this job now or no job at all. But it's not your fault, Doug. Not unless you knew what she was up to."

He shook his head. "She must've really wanted you here. And, honestly, I get it. After seeing you dance today, I was ready to bang you over the head and drag you back to my cave, if you pardon my French."

I chuckled. "Lots of that going around, it seems. Your schmuck boss seems to be of the same persuasion."

That got his attention real quick. "Did he do something? Because I'll kick his ass."

I bit the inside of my cheek. Both us getting fired in the span of one day would be way too much. I shook my head and shrugged. "He just comes off as…intense. You know?"

"Yeah. People here often do."

Which reminded me. "Is Justine into the whole spanky-spanky thing?"

He snorted. "I think she's more into the whippy-whippy thing, getting or giving side. Why?"

Hmmm. "Is mister schmuck-boss into that too?" I could definitely see Anthony Gowl playing master to someone. He'd probably get a surreal kick out of taking care of some sweet little pet-thing.

"That I don't know. Justine plays around in the club, but Gowl rarely shows up. He might be in his office doing the kinky every night for all I know, but he rarely comes out. Whatever Tony's pleasure is, he seems to keep it pretty private."

I grinned. "Be honest with me. Do you change into leather pants in there? Because I could almost pay to see you in some."

He pinched my shoulder and started up the car. "Smartass," he whispered. "I hear your costume made a killing tonight. I'll stop by next time and see you do your thing, doll."

"Promises, promises. Why didn't you come see me tonight?"

He sighed, ran a hand over his bald head. "Tough night, doll. I had to throw one obnoxious asshole out of the Playroom and get him banned."

His profile looked so…strong. Doug gave me the distinct impression of a mountain. I wondered how the other guy looked.

"What did he do?"

"Didn't stop when he was asked to, the little shit."

I shivered. "Does that mean he—"

"He hurt the one he was playing with. There's a zero-tolerance policy on these asshats."

The thought horrified me. But then again, I was a patented coward. Obviously, there were people brave—or maybe foolish?—enough to put their trust in people to such an extent that they'd become powerless. It took balls of steel to do that, I thought, no matter who was doing it. Balls I seriously lacked. I shook my head. Who was I kidding? I was terrified of a guy because he made me want him.

"I'll come see you dance tomorrow, doll. Provided things don't go insane again."

"You do that. So you'll come over when it's time to go? Like, eight-ish?"

"You got it."

When we arrived home, he waited for me to get into my apartment and close the door before he went into his. I washed up, cleaned my face of all the makeup, and crashed asleep.

• • •

Noise exploded around me. Loud, annoying. I groaned and turned the other way, dug my head into the pillow. No use— the horrible noise kept up. I picked up my phone, looked at the screen. Nothing. That wasn't it. There was no other phone, no alarm clock. What the hell? Knocking joined in. Ugh. Could that be the doorbell? I didn't even know I had one. I dragged myself out of bed and heard some voices on the hall. Just as I was ready to head back to bed the knocking resumed.

"Jesus freaking Christ, yes! I'm comin—"

I froze there. Right before me stood tall, gorgeous, and annoying Anthony Gowl. And he was grinning.

"Is this a nightmare?" I muttered under my breath.

"Judging by your sleepwear, more of a fantasy. But I'm awake, so I don't know what that makes this."

I frowned and looked down. My sleepwear was a pair of shorts and a top. Well, not showing more skin than the costumes. "What's wrong with my sleepwear?"

"Not a thing. But it looks so…intimate. I like your morning look. Truly beautiful women are beautiful right when they wake up."

I snorted. "Whatever. You clearly know nothing of women if you think that. Now what are you doing here?"

"Will you let me in, or are we talking on the hall?"

I thought about it. The only other person living here was Doug, so I was sort of okay talking in the door like that. But he just looked so hopeful, like a puppy. I almost felt bad to keep him there. So I shrugged and turned around, heading for the kitchen. "I'm making coffee. Want some?"

The door clicked closed behind him. "Sure, thanks."

"Sit down or whatever," I called over my shoulder.

Once the coffee was all done, I poured two mugs of it and brought them into the living room. He'd settled down on the couch, coat shrugged off. He wore chocolate brown pants and a lovely, crisp, white shirt. Not clean-shaven like he'd been the night before, and I sort of liked this look better. There was something about men with a maximum of three days' growth that was incredibly sexy. I left his mug on the coffee table and walked into the bedroom, put on a pair of sweats. Sitting with him on my couch, him in a suit and me in shorts just seemed wrong on so many levels.

"Don't dress up on my account. I liked your earlier outfit—"

I held up my hand and took a few gulps of coffee. The nectar of the gods slid down my throat and made me incredibly happy. I truly woke up then, my brain getting its gears in motion.

I sighed with delight then fixed my eyes on him. "Okay, now I'm ready to begin the day. What the hell are you doing here?"

"I think I liked you better before the coffee. You were so soft and pliable…"

I squinted my eyes and took another gulp. "Start talking or I'm calling Doug to throw you out."

"Nice, but he won't. I just talked to him on the phone and he's not here right now, so unless you somehow manage to throw out a man probably three times your size, I'm not going anywhere."

"Charming. Again, what are you doing here?"

He put his coffee mug on the table and leaned in a bit. Bad news was written all over his face. I knew that look. I'd seen it often enough.

"What's wrong?" I asked, resigned.

"Tina was beaten up late last night as she was going home. Badly beaten up."

As much as I didn't like her on account of going blabber-mouth on me with Sam, I sort of liked the woman overall. The thought of that beautiful face all swollen up made me sick. But Anthony and I—or Justine and I for that matter—weren't close friends or anything. There was no real reason to come over and tell me about it unless I was somehow involved. And there was only way I could have been involved, as far as I could see. I inspected his face, the grim determination there.

"You think it was Sam."

He nodded. "He's a good-for-nothing piece of shit, and Tina did say he took the news of your departure rather…personally. Threatened her and whatnot."

What had she been thinking when she went over to gloat in his face about stealing one of his moneymakers? I shook my head, settled back in the cushions. "Yeah, he's a shit, all right. But I can't see him going as far as beating up a girl over it. I mean…I don't know, did she go to the police?"

This time he shook his head. "She'd rather not. Her life is, well, complicated I guess. Police snooping around wouldn't be in her best interests right now, she says. I tried to talk some sense into her but she's pretty stubborn."

I nibbled on the inside of my cheek. "I thought she was a sub?"

He frowned, eyes going ice cold. "So you think she got off on getting beaten?"

"No, asshole! I thought she wouldn't be so stubborn, especially around someone as annoying and pushy as you."

He inspected me for a few seconds more, then sighed. "Look, I'm sorry. I haven't slept at all and after seeing her like that…I'm sorry. I jumped to conclusions. But she's one of the most stubborn women I know. What she does in the Playroom is just one facet of her personality."

"Can't you, I don't know, find out? I mean if it was Sam, I'm sure Doug would *love* to talk to him about it."

He smiled and leaned back into the couch. "I'm sure he would, but she made him promise not to. If it was Sam, that would mean you're next. I have it on good authority his high-rollers up and left last night when they found out you weren't there anymore."

"They did?"

I hated how cheerful I sounded, but there was some pride in the fact they'd been loyal to me in the end. That they were still mine, in a way. Maybe I was a horrible person for thinking it, especially under the circumstances, but it brought me pleasure to know that.

"Why would I be next, though?"

His eyes turned assessing. I didn't like it, not one bit.

"You better spit it out, Anthony. Don't go all Daddy on me. It's going to end badly if you try."

He sighed. "Tony called to let me know. The guy likes you, doesn't want to see you hurt. He called and said you should look out for a while."

"So he knows Sam beat up Justine?"

"He didn't say as much, but it's pretty clear how things stand."

My shoulders slumped. "Great. That means Doug will probably move in here and start building defense lines all over my living room."

He pushed one finger under my chin, made me meet his eyes. "No, he won't. I'd like you to move in with me until I sort this out."

My eyes went saucer-wide. "What?"

"I'm responsible for your safety. It was Tina's lack of finesse that pissed him off to begin with. I'm not saying it's her fault any of this happened—it's that asshole Sam's fault, of course. But I feel responsible, anyway. So I'd like you to consider this. Doug thinks it's the best idea, too. This is not exactly a secure building, and Doug might not be here a lot. He'll spend a lot of time with Tina while she recovers, so we'd both feel better to know you're safe."

Sam was a complete asshole, that much I knew. He tended to go raving mad and throw things around, maybe get into it with Tony over things. But I couldn't really see him beating up a woman. Then again, I would never have thought my father would stab my mom thirty-four times then kill himself over her body, so what did I know? I didn't know this guy, either. He had shifty eyes that inspired in me no confidence. The worst part was there was a thick shadow wrapped around him, something dark and dangerous, and it scared and also turned me on a little. He was the first guy I responded to that way. That in itself was reason enough to turn tail and run as fast as I could. It was the ones you really liked, the ones who got close enough, who'd hurt you the most. I knew that for a fact.

"Maybe I could stay with Justine?" I wondered out loud.

He shook his head, ran a hand through his hair. I felt bad about liking his distressed look, but I liked it nonetheless.

"She's not…easy to deal with right now. She and Doug have known each other for a while. You're nice and everything, but you just met and she's—"

I nodded. "Hurt. She trusts Doug, doesn't trust me to be around her. I get it, I totally do. But the thing is, it's the same for me. I mean, I just met you, you're more or less tolerable and all but—"

"But you don't trust me."

I shrugged. "Don't take it personally. I have issues trusting people. The fact you've been hitting on me doesn't help things, either. Plus this is going all—"

"Daddy on you. I thought you'd say that."

I really hated his habit of not letting me finish my goddamn sentences. He blinked a few times, those gorgeous dark eyes of his going murky. He was beautiful in a way that was hard to pinpoint. His face wasn't model-like; he had thick, dark eyebrows to match the dark hair. His eyes were almost black and always disconcertingly hungry as he looked at me. He had plush lips but not too big, though his mouth seemed a bit wide for his Roman nose. I liked the sturdy line of his jaw, though. The strong neck, too, and most of all his body. Tall and wide, intimidating. An air of power buzzed around him. It would make perfect sense to me if he was a Dom. He certainly seemed the type and seemed to have the instincts to go owner-mode on someone he liked.

There was a fine line between what scared me and what attracted me. Richie was a big guy too, and I found Doug attractive—he was as big as one could get. But Richie had a very chilled-out personality, he wasn't clingy or possessive, and that made me feel safe around him. Doug was very in-your-face protective about me, but he had a good sense of the lines between us and didn't step over; if and when he did, he quickly took the step back and fell into comfortable territory. It went unsaid between us, but I trusted him because of that.

This guy, though—I had no idea what to make of him. He loved to push my barriers, my lines of defense. He loved to provoke me, then he stepped back just as I was ready to push, only to go right back to pushing before I could recover. It didn't feel like a brutal invasion as much as a snake slithering around the perimeter. Like he was waiting to catch me in a moment of weakness and slide around my body to choke me. It sent chills up my spine but provoked me into playing his game too, at least up to a point. And that was what worried me the most. He had a way of getting me playful instead of defensive. He might actually get too close because I wasn't on full alert to poke him away when I should. I couldn't do that kind of close; he had to be at least arm's length away. He wouldn't be able to stab me in the back that way. The thought made me shiver.

"I could move in with you, make sure you're not alone. But Sam knows where you live, and it's a lot safer if you stay at my place. Someone could break in here easy as pie. My place, however…it's a bit harder to break into."

I saw the logic in that. It didn't make me trust him any more, but there was logic. I thought about calling Tony, but he hadn't called to let me know about Sam's rampage-mode. Maybe he had good reason for that, so calling him might work against me. I scrubbed a hand over my face.

"I had such an easy life two days ago. I already miss that. This is all just crazy."

"I'm sorry things went this way. But I'll work things out, I promise you that."

"That doesn't give me a lot of confidence. Too daddy."

He chuckled and leaned in, gaze running over my face. "I have a tendency to be protective, so sue me. Isn't everyone protective of people they like or care about?"

"There's a fine line between protective and possessive, if you ask me. I've seen it crossed and end in disaster."

"Was your dad very protective of you?"

I froze. "Why are you asking about my father?"

"Daddy issues tend to be connected to a daddy. It's either the dad or some long-term relationship, but I think you're too young for the latter. So it must be a Daddy-daddy issue. Isn't it?"

I swallowed thickly and took a few gulps of coffee. This was entirely the wrong topic of discussion for the morning—or for the day or night, either. "Are you sure you want me to stay over at your place? What will your woman think about that?"

"Fine, you don't want to talk about it. We will when you're ready. And do you really think I'm involved if I'm hitting on you, as you put it?"

I shrugged. At this point I was ready to start packing just to get his mind off the previous topic of discussion. I went for my phone in the bedroom, sat on the bed, and called Doug.

"Hey doll, you all right?" he asked.

"Hey. Yeah, so Anthony Gowl is standing here in my living room demanding I go over to his place for a while."

"I know. I'm at Justine's now."

"How is she?"

He sighed. "Doesn't look pretty, I hate to say. That bastard did a number on her."

"I don't understand why he'd react this way. I mean…"

"Someone came into his turf, took one of his girls, and then flaunted the fact in his face. He needs to reaffirm he's top dog or he'll lose cred."

"Jesus Christ, I was just a goddamn dancer! Not like someone stole his kingdom or something."

Dough laughed. "You're clueless sometimes, doll. There's more than dancing going on in the Pearl, and losing cred isn't good for Sam's business."

I knew, but I went along with it as if I didn't. "Clearly, I'm missing something. So you think I should do what this guy Anthony says? Do you trust him?"

"It's your best bet right now as I see it. If he does anything funny, you just tell me. I'm dying to throw some punches around. At this point, anyone who gives me a reason will do."

I breathed in deep. "Okay. Okay, I'll go. Send Justine my best."

"Will do."

As he disconnected, I looked up. Anthony leaned against the doorframe, wide shoulders in gorgeous full display. Checking him out was probably not a good idea, considering I was staying over at his place for a while. I had a very bad feeling about the whole situation.

"Did you get Doug's approval?" he asked with a lazy smile on his face.

I frowned and looked away. "Jealous?"

Anthony walked over and sat on the bed beside me. "A little. Grab whatever you'll need for a few days and let's move. I'd like to have you settled in before we have to get to work today. I always go over to the club around seven—you mind if we go there together then?"

I shrugged. "No, not really. Beats getting the key to your place."

I blushed and stared into my lap. This conversation seemed so much more intimate than it was. Me moving in, getting keys, us going to work together. Entirely too chummy for my liking.

"Hey," he whispered. "You're going to be fine. We'll work this out and everything will go back to normal, okay? Don't worry."

"Right. So I should worry enough to move in with you for a few days, but not worry a lot, huh?"

He chuckled and I joined in. Pretty ridiculous, but then again I never did get to do things the easy way.

My dad's parents used to own a big monster of a Rottweiler named Rex. Everyone outside the family was downright terrified of him. I guess they had good reason to. But he loved to hang around me. I used to play horsie with him, in fact. I'd get up on his back, and he'd strut around the backyard like I was a prize he'd gotten. I remember he had jaws big enough to swallow my head, but I wasn't really scared of him. He did inspire a certain brand of respect, true. But I also wanted to spend time with him and play horsie.

This guy was sort of like that. He looked big and scary and inspired a lot of respect. And yet I wanted to spend time with him…and play horsie, I guessed.

Chapter 6

When we got to Anthony's place, a few things became clear. One—he was a security freak. His building was full of cameras, alarm systems, and shit. I'd been right—there was something seriously wrong with people who had pristine white floors. There was also something substantially wrong with people who wired up their living space like Fort Knox. Two—that club of his was doing way better than I'd thought. He lived in a duplex the size of a freaking warehouse. Three—there was something going on between Justine and him. They lived in the same building but different apartments. There had to be something going on, right? Then again, I lived in the same building as Doug, so maybe they were just friends. I found the topic entirely too interesting. A very bad sign—a girl didn't get that curious unless she was interested. I didn't want to be interested, but then again I rarely got what I wanted.

"I think you'll have to give me a raise so I can afford rent here," I mumbled.

He turned around after dropping his keys on a bar in the living room area. "We haven't really discussed how much you'll make. And if you think you're paying me rent, you're delusional."

I squinted my eyes and stabbed a finger in his direction. "You're not my friend, so stop acting like we're buddies. If I'm living in your place for a few days, I'm paying rent. It's either that or I turn around and walk right out of Fort Knox here."

He sighed as his beautifully large body dropped into a chair. "You know, when you act like a petulant teenager it's hard not go all daddy-mode on you."

"Fuck you," I said, smiling like an angel.

It backfired on me. He grinned and his eyes instantly turned hotter. "I'd love you to. Thanks for the offer. It's settled, then— you pay me rent in hot, sweaty, monkey sex."

My face heated up and I crossed my hands over my chest. "It wasn't an offer. Don't pretend to be denser than you are."

"Shouldn't have said it if you didn't mean it. Too late now. You can't unspeak the words."

I turned around and pointedly walked to the door. In three seconds flat a bunch of things went wrong. A shadow loomed over mine, which was a sign I was in trouble. Next, a body came hairpin close to mine. Worst, I reached the door, grabbed the handle, and that body behind me closed a big paw over my hand and pressed me against the door. The bag with my stuff fell from my hand and I froze, mind going entirely blank. I shivered as cold sweat trailed down my spine.

"Don't run away, Beatrice. It'll only make me chase you all the harder."

I blinked repeatedly and franticly searched my brain for some coherent speech. I came up short. Instead of telling him to go fuck himself, for instance, I just stood there with stiff muscles and cold sweat trickling down my body. My heart pounded like crazy, breath shallow. Freak-out was just around the corner.

"Beatrice?" he asked in a mellow voice.

I didn't respond, so he slowly turned me around, gripping both my arms. Being face-to-face made everything worse, because I could actually see him closing in on me, all tall and wide and much too close. I shivered and pushed against the door—and that didn't help any. I was trapped there, overpowered. I felt the haze wrap around my brain, fight or flight starting to zing through my muscles. Just as I was about to start flailing and screaming like a banshee the huge body before me knelt.

It was surprising enough to make me look down. Watching him go down on his knees before me flipped a switch in my head. The pounding heart turned into a throbbing body, and I was turned on as easy as that. I sucked in a deep breath.

"What are you doing?" I croaked.

"I'm not trying to cage you, sparrow. Don't flutter away."

I looked down into burning hot eyes, stared at the line of his lips. The hands on my arms felt reverent instead of intrusive, and my spine heated up, shooting bolts of warmth through my body. Anthony Gowl on his knees was the most erotic thing I'd ever seen. I licked my lips and enjoyed that feeling, the slow power vibe wrapping around my stomach, coating my heart. He was my fan right then. I had him. He was mine to tease, mine to feed on, mine to deny. And the thought brought a tidal wave of satisfaction through me.

I lifted a hand slowly and planted it in his hair, fingers spread wide and combing through the rich, dark mass. Little crackles of electricity sparked to life where my palm touched his scalp. Something sticky and sweet possessed me as I pulled on his hair and watched his lips part on a breath.

"What are you trying to do, Anthony?" I asked in low voice.

He licked his lips and caressed me with his thumbs, his hands still holding mine. Warmth spread through my body, and a new round of shivers traveled up my spine, not cold ones this time. God help me, I really wanted him right then.

"I want you to want me, sparrow. I want you to have me any way you'll take it. I can't stop thinking about you since last night."

I inhaled deeply, and my chest shuddered with the weight of his words. We both knew he was still the one pushing, but it didn't feel like. It didn't make me freak out, even though it was a game. But he knew how to play me at this game, and I found that shamefully exciting. I had to clear my head, dissolve the effect he had on me.

"If I'm going to stay here, hooking up isn't the best idea."

He didn't even blink, just stared into my eyes in that intoxicating way and kept giving me that bubbly flutter in my stomach.

"If you're sleepy, you'll use the bed. If you want to wash, you'll use the shower. Think of me that way, if that's what it takes. Use me. I want to be used by you if it means I can touch you. I don't need to be in charge here, sparrow. I just want to touch you so bad right now…"

I licked my lips and started massaging his scalp. For freak's sake, why did that turn me on so goddamn bad?

"You want to be the instrument of my pleasure?" I rasped.

He nodded, rubbing his thumbs against my skin in slow circles. It was a bad idea, a really bad one, but it had been a while…and I missed feeling not alone. I knew as I made the decision that it was a really bad one, but right then my mind wasn't really doing the driving. The throbbing blood in my veins was in charge. The surge of warmth between my legs was in charge. And I gave in. Looking down at him, I licked my lips slowly and loved the flutter of his chest as he watched my tongue move.

"Get my shoes off," I whispered.

I lifted one foot and then the other, watching him with rapt attention as his hands slid my flats off. His fingers caressed the soles of my feet. His touch tickled, but as soon as it felt really ticklish he'd rub his fingers against my soles in a way that shot right up between my legs. I pressed my lips shut, afraid I might actually moan. He slid his fingers against my skin again, pushed slowly from under my toes to my ankles. God, how could that feel so good?

"Pants," I whispered.

He spread his palms wide on each side of my ankles and slowly rubbed them up my legs, applying enough pressure that I would feel it but not enough to feel like I was being grabbed. I shivered when he finally reached my hips and hooked his fingers into the elastic of my sweats. He pulled them down in that same excruciatingly slow way, running his palms over skin as it was exposed. I stepped out of them once they were finally down and shuddered as he bent to kiss my knees, rubbing his hot lips against the sensitive skin at the side of each. My clit throbbed. I was wet and slippery already, impatient to be touched.

"Panties," I said so low I feared he might not hear.

But he did. His dark eyes sparked with hunger, fixed on mine as his palms rubbed slowly up my legs from ankle to hip again. My heart thumped harshly as he hooked his fingers into the band of my panties, and he didn't blink as he slowly dragged them down to my feet. My knees almost buckled as air rushed against my bare skin. I had to brace myself on his shoulders, not trusting to stay up on my own. Sweet Jesus, he hadn't even touched me properly yet.

Once my panties went the way of the sweats, he stared up, palms running over my legs but not brushing higher than my thighs. My skin pebbled along with my nipples.

"What do you want me to do now, sparrow?" he rumbled.

Mmm, that voice crawled all over me like a hot, slick tongue. Fire burned though my veins, impatient and demanding. "Get naked and lie down on the couch there."

He made to get up but I pushed the tips of my nails into his shoulders and he stopped.

"Don't walk, crawl."

His eyes flashed up at me. I got the tingles all over and the hotness in his eyes almost drowned me. He slowly unbuttoned his shirt and threw it off. His skin looked as delicious as I'd imagined, smooth and tan enough to make me want to lick it and see it shine. Dark hair was sprinkled over his chest, and it crawled down firm abs to point at the tent in his pants. I licked my lips quickly as he opened his belt. The clicks of metal as the belt parted and the hiss of his zipper as he opened it were music to my ears.

"Sit back. Let me take them off." I spoke thickly.

He smiled as he crawled back on the floor, going into the direction of the couch. I loved the way his hips moved and how his round ass flexed with each movement. He stood, his legs spread. His pants hung open and inviting like a present, and I was dying to unwrap him. I gripped the hem of my T-shirt and threw it away. The bra underneath quickly followed. By the time I reached his feet, I was completely naked and flushed all over, I was that turned on.

He grinned, and I clasped both pants legs and pulled. They slid off easily. He looked good enough to eat, all muscles and strength. His skin sang for me as I touched him, burning hot and firm. I stared at the bulge in his black briefs and thought of Christmas mornings. This was like winning at a lottery, and I really wanted to tear into my prize.

"Get on the couch, sitting position."

He crawled over to it, giving me a good view of his beautifully round ass. My mind clouded over entirely when he finally sat there, leaning back, naked and gorgeous. And in that insane moment of zero rationality, he seemed almost mine. I stalked over and straddled his lap, smoothly set my core on the bulging fabric of his briefs. The warmth of his body spread through me. I pushed myself against his chest, tucked my head in the crook of his neck.

"You're wet," he whispered against my ear.

I arched my spine and began to rub against him slowly. He groaned and I bit my lip, the slow movement of my hips frustrating and exhilarating at the same time. His hands closed around my hips and I shuddered, biting his ear harshly. He hissed but ground my hips down hard, very hard against him. The hard shape of him pushed up against my wet folds and I swallowed thickly.

"I want to feel you," he said against my ear.

My heart pounded hard enough to make my ears zing. I wanted to feel him, too. But not yet. "Touch me. Touch me anywhere you'd like, just don't close your hands around me."

His fingers flexed hard on my hips, then one of them glided around to grip one buttock. He rubbed his hand all over it, made my spine tingle from my backbone up. His other hand slid up my stomach to wrap around the underside of my breast, massaging and gripping enough to make me arch back. His hands felt hard and hungry on me, strong. But I didn't wig out; I got hotter because of it. He kept rubbing and twisting at me until I moaned against his ear, my hips rubbing down hard against his bulge all the while.

I shivered as one of his palms rubbed its way up from the small of my back to my nape. My skin got goose bumped all over, and I screeched into his throat. Hot, so hot. I needed him inside me.

I pulled away, lifted my hips from him. His hands gripped hard, trying to keep me in place.

"Let go."

"You're driving me insane here," he rasped.

I chuckled and kissed his cheek. "Condom?"

He sighed with obvious relief, his bones going liquid underneath me. "Back pocket of my pants."

I got up and walked over to where I'd tossed them. Three condoms. Perfect. I liked a man who needed more than the emergency one. I allowed my gaze to lick over him, straining hard and clad in briefs as he was. My juices were on him already. I loved the thought of that. I walked over slowly, put the condoms on the couch beside him. I was feeling brave, braver than ever before. More powerful as his eyes were glued to mine. I knelt before him and watched his chest expand. He spread his knees to fit me between them and I licked my lips, looking up.

"Lift your hips. I'm taking these off."

His abs flexed as he pushed off the couch. I pulled the briefs down to his thighs, pushing his knees closer together with my own legs so I could easily pull them off when he sat back down. I loved the dark hair on his legs, loved the way it brushed against my bare skin. Once the briefs were off, I knelt between his knees again, ran my hands up his thighs all the way to his hipbones. His muscles quivered under my touch, and his hard-on jumped when I was close enough to touch. But I didn't.

Instead, I looked up at him, took in the way his lids were half-closed as he stared down. He wanted me so much right then that his eyes were trying to pull me inside him, to suck my soul in and devour it. No one had ever felt as powerful under my hands as he did, and the tingling rush that feeling brought me was new, dark, and delicious. It danced on the edge of scaring me, a flickering flame that ran playfully over my nerve endings.

"You love torturing me, don't you?" he said with a small smile.

I didn't. I shook my head slowly and grabbed the condoms, tearing open one of the packs.

"Not torturing you. Just giving myself time to adjust. You're just sitting there, all good and pliable," I said, grinning.

His eyes flashed dangerously, and I sat back down on my haunches immediately. He blinked once and the edge was gone, the hotness from before sizzling back into place.

"And yet you're still so intimidating I might run away any moment," I admitted.

"I'm intimidating to you?"

I nodded and got closer, condom in my hand. I gripped his hot length and put the condom at the very tip of him, but before going any farther I looked up and swallowed thickly.

"If you hold on to me too tight I might freak out. If I do freak out, you have to promise you'll let me go. Not rush in on me."

His eyes turned unbearably sad for a moment but he nodded solemnly. Which was sort of funny since he was butt naked and straining hard in my hand. But I appreciated the commitment. He sucked in air as I slid the condom in place, cupping the coated and slick length of him when I was done. Making eye contact, I crawled up in his lap and straddled him, keeping my hips up, and fixed my hands on his big shoulders for balance.

"I want you inside me," I whispered, looking into his beautiful eyes.

He smiled softly, gripped himself, and positioned his tip at my entrance. I circled my hips slowly, keeping him there, then I shot down his length and gasped at how perfectly filled I felt. He groaned and gripped my hip tight with one hand, the other rubbing against the underside of my other thigh. I shivered and circled my hips on him again, earning another groan. He felt perfect inside me, hot and big and hard. I rubbed my lips against his. They trembled, and I just knew he was dying to plunge inside my mouth. But he didn't, and I admired him for the effort. I wanted to repay it, too, so I blew out a gust of hot air against his lips before speaking.

"You can kiss me, you know."

He groaned, frustrated. I loved to feel him so tense, his yearning pulsing so beautifully through his body. He was like a raging storm kept in tight wraps, the raging power inside him crawling all over my skin and rubbing at my nipples. I brushed my lips against his, opened my mouth, and kissed him softly. His lips parted for me, and I pushed inside him with my tongue, caressed him and coaxed a response. He made me work for it, though he pulsed hard inside me with desire.

I began to move my hips in a mad rhythm, the rhythm he created inside of me through the beats of my heart. His taste spread through my mouth, fresh and minty but hot as hell. His hunger grew; he pushed harder into my lips and I held strong, allowing him to take more. He'd given me so much already. I wanted to give back as much as I could. His hand kept a firm grip on my hip, but the other one wrapped around my cheek and pulled me in deeper, held me there for him to feed from. I whimpered but increased the rhythm of my hips, letting him know this was good.

I could do this, though that tingle of almost-fear kept tickling at the edges of my pleasure. He devoured me, the way he kissed betraying the hunger I'd felt in him all along. Thick, endless hunger, burgeoning and hot just like the length of him rubbing inside me. I shook and rode him harder, almost frantically. My insides adjusted to accommodate him better, his strokes hitting me deeper than my body. I moaned into his mouth and his grip became harder, more demanding. The wave of pleasure surged higher, stronger than anything I'd ever felt before. At the edges of it frothed the tingle of fear, of losing control.

I fought against it, suddenly scared but unable, unwilling to stop playing on that edge. He groaned thickly into my mouth and began to push into me from beneath with hard, almost punishing strokes that kept up with my frantic rhythm. He never let go, not once, didn't ease his grip. That wave of pleasure quickly turned into a tsunami. All my fears, all my pleasures, all my worries, everything I'd ever felt or dreaded mixed into one single massive wall, and when it crashed through me I screamed and shook brutally on top of him. He held on to my hip and my face and pushed deep inside, finding his own release.

Waves of aftershocks tingled through my body, and he finally pulled his mouth away from mine. I fell against his chest, both of us panting hard enough to fill the big room. Sweat glided down my body, hot and wet friction between us. In my muddled state of mind, I buried my forehead into his neck and took in greedy gulps of his scent. My body shook a few times more as he ran his hands over my sweaty skin.

And I knew right then that I was in way over my head. I was unable to run away—it washed through me with crystal clarity. His grip on my body, stone hard, said he wouldn't let go. And I was doomed.

Chapter 7

I shivered as sweat turned cold on my body. His fingers still burned where they kept a solid grip. My heart squeezed tight and my stomach fluttered.

"This was a mistake," I mumbled into his skin.

He sighed. "Don't say that when I'm still inside you."

I rubbed my face against him harder and stood there wishing for…something. I wasn't sure what. I wanted to feel him around me, and it scared the hell out of me. My jaws clenched as I tried to say something, to ask for whatever it was I needed. I had no idea what that was. He pushed his head into the crook of my neck, giving me a small embrace of sorts without using his hands. I shivered as I inhaled and exhaled, all my air rich with the smell of him. He was what my blood carried though my body right then, what sustained me.

"I'm scared," I whispered.

And as the words came out, I didn't know if I wanted him to really hear them or not. Because if he did, he'd ask why. And I might not be able to avoid answering him. He'd have a power over me I didn't allow anyone else to have. Not since my parents… died. It was the power of knowing what truly filled me with fear, and once someone knew that then they could find ways to use it to get me, to dig inside me deep enough I wouldn't be able to pull away anymore. It would leave me defenseless, vulnerable. I couldn't stand that thought. It made me shiver. I stood there, all my muscles clenched and tension radiating from me despite just having had the best sex of my life.

He didn't ask me, though. I wasn't sure how I felt about that—if I was relieved or disappointed. Maybe both. He'd have to care to ask, and why would he care? We'd just met a day ago, and I'd already slept with him. Not much of a challenge there anymore, was there? Partly why I'd done it. Men didn't chase after something if they got it easily enough—they didn't hold on to what was already theirs. It was what belonged to someone else or what refused itself to them that they wanted. It was the challenge, the pissing contest that got them going. I slumped there in his arms so he'd know there was no challenge here anymore. He'd had the free and untouchable dancer he'd wanted the night before. So now he'd back off, I told myself. He'd be kind, maybe friendly, but move on. And the thought both scared and pleased me.

"I'm scared that things will turn ugly between us now. We'll work together so I want us to be on good terms."

He pulled back, eyes turning hard. So quickly, too. He'd turned cold so quickly after having me. Maybe I'd disappointed him, presented too little of a challenge for him to feel any satisfaction now everything was over.

"Just how big of a slime-ball do you take me for?"

I pulled away too, blinked a few times. Why did it matter what I thought of him at this point? His gaze jumped over my face, and his thick brows furrowed almost comically.

"You're the most frustrating woman I know, and I've just known you for one day. I shudder to think how far up the wall you'll drive me by the end of the week."

I casually pinched his nipple and felt him twitch inside me. He sighed and reached over to kiss my cheek, disentangling himself from under me. I watched him disappear behind a door, his gorgeous, naked body making me blush. He came back a few minutes later still naked and so beautifully male, so powerful and intimidating in the buff that I bit the inside of my cheek until I tasted copper. Thing was, I wanted him all over again. But I wasn't about to mention that when I didn't know what was going on in his head. My eyes trailed down to his package, and I grinned despite myself. What was going on in his other head? Because that one was pretty easy to figure out at this point.

He reached out a hand to me and smiled, dark eyes dancing with a giddiness I felt stirring in the pit of my stomach.

"Let me give you the full tour. I like how well you took to the living room."

I rolled my eyes at him and walked over. Trying to make it seem as casual as the Sunday paper, I slipped my hand in his and shivered a bit when he closed his fingers around it. My heart jumped around in my chest when he pulled me in closer and reached out to caress my face. I fully expected to freeze somewhere on the way there, the freak-out maybe. Touching him felt way too intimate. Sleeping with Richie felt less intimate than Anthony holding my hand. It was a clear warning flag if I'd ever seen one, but I found myself miserably unable to pull back right then. He'd let go, though, I reasoned with myself. He'd get bored and let go, and I'd be safe. I could enjoy the temporary insanity in the meantime. The thought thrilled and terrified me, a mix I had begun to associate with him. It was a heady, powerful mix. One I'd never thought to enjoy, yet here I was, burning up to have him inside me again. Chemistry like that was hard to escape.

We went up the stairs, my hand in his. He had two bedrooms, his and a guest room. We went into his, him leading as he walked backward. When we reached the edge of his bed he grinned and pulled me closer to him, eyes going hungry all over again.

"Aren't you forgetting something?" I asked, smiling.

"Hmmm…condoms?"

I nodded. He grinned brighter. "We have a whole pack of them up here, no worries. Those were my emergency stash," he said, chuckling. "I'm delighted we had an 'emergency.'"

I chuckled and looked up at him, my nipples still hard.

"Can I be on top this time?" he whispered huskily.

I froze and swallowed thickly, stepped back, pulling to get my hand free of his. "N-no. I can't—"

He stepped back a bit but still held my hand, hooked a finger under my chin to angle my face back up. "Don't rush to fly away, sparrow. It's okay. I loved you on top."

I breathed in deeply and kept staring up into his eyes. There was a warmth there I hadn't noticed before, a kind of generosity that went straight into my heart. He was willing to give me as much space as he could, and yet he was still holding my hand. It wasn't the kind of space Richie gave me—Richie was perfectly happy with getting up and going home after we had sex, never lingering to make me uncomfortable or push to get anything beyond what I gave him. But it felt like he simply didn't want more of me, and that was what made him so safe.

Right now, with Anthony, it felt like he was compromising. Like he wanted more, like he needed more of me, but was willing to settle with this much because it was how much I had to give right then. My chest tingled because of it, but my stomach was a tight ball of nerves too. He kept me on that edge. And he did that all just by holding my hand or looking into my eyes. My skin rose in goose bumps again, and I stepped closer to him, craving his body heat.

"I want to taste you," he whispered against the top of my head.

I smiled and reached my mouth up to his, curling my toes as he kissed me. But he pulled away smiling, lips still wet. His hand slid between my legs and cupped me.

"I want to taste you here."

I shivered and ran the tip of my tongue against his nipple. He hummed in appreciation and I bit it, sucking it hard into my mouth. When the hard nub was wet and throbbing I pulled back, satisfied.

"Lay back on the bed, big boy."

He grinned as he did, propping up on his elbows. I stood up on the bed, one foot on each side of his body, legs parted enough to give him a teaser but not a full view. He put his hands down on the bed, looking up at me with enough craving to make my clit tingle.

"You're so beautiful. Will you let me taste you?" he whispered.

I bit my lip and stepped up to his head, bending my knees slowly to straddle his neck. He licked his lips and brought the palms of his hands to the backs of my thighs, rubbing softly. I sucked in a breath and closed the distance, straddling his face but keeping my hips up. He arched his neck and buried his head between my legs, pulled at my thighs to lower my hips enough for him to reach with ease. I sucked in shuddering breaths as he lapped at me, nibbled softly on my folds, and sucked my clit into his mouth. My hips shuddered and began to sway over his face, spurring his hunger on. I bit my lower lip hard and bent over to press my hands against the mattress above his head. The orgasm came quickly and left my insides throbbing. He did this to me; he ripped me free from my hold. He kept lapping at me tenderly as my hips shook, and by the time I crawled down his body he was straining hard.

"Where are those famous condoms of yours?"

He licked his lips like a cat after drinking milk, obvious satisfaction radiating from his every pore. "Nightstand, right side. Top drawer."

I leaned over to pry it open, rummaging through it blindly as his lips got busy on my nipples. By the time I finally reached the damn pack, I was ready to sing hymns of joy. I tore into one while he chuckled at my brutality. I crawled down his body to put the condom on him. But before I did, I took the time to lick very slowly and wetly at his length, paying special attention to the slit on his bulging head. His hips tried to push against me so I held him down and *tsked*. He actually laughed and groaned with frustration at the same time, which was inexplicably cute. Once I was satisfied with how much I'd teased his impatient flesh, I rolled the condom over him and settled my core against his tip.

This time I wasn't rushing at all. I thrust myself down with steel resolve and swayed my hips on him decisively but in slow motion. Each time he began to thrust up, I leaned down and gripped his base tightly, pulling groans from him but buying more time too. His hips soon stopped trying to rush me, a strange look of annoyance and fascination settling into his eyes. He crossed his hands under his head; I wasn't sure if it was to stop himself from grabbing me or to better enjoy the show. Sweat covered both our bodies, his muscles rippling with every movement of my hips. But I had no mercy to spare. I gripped the base of him and did my very best to make sure I'd be dancing on top of him for a good while. Each time the wave threatened to drown me I'd slow down, sway around more, buy myself more time. His lips would tighten in a straight line, eyes slightly squinting. It turned me on all the more to see him pissed off but still holding those hands under his head.

After I had my fill of that beauty radiating from his face, I began to thrust down with more purpose, reaching over to pinch at his nipples to the rhythm of my hips. He threw his head back, neck tendons straining and arms bulging with his need to come. I loved to see him there, hovering right at the edge of bliss. I threw myself deeper into the rhythm of his need, pinched his nipples harder with each thrust as moans spilled from my mouth like a chant. Good, so good…He filled me perfectly, his body so strong as it coiled tight under me. The rush of pleasure tingled through my entire body, a persistent throb that slowly speared me, gathering between my legs. I fell on him with abandon as I came, gripping him inside tightly. I felt like I was drowning in pleasure. He made a mewling sound as he arched up and drove himself deep into me, coming hard and shivering as I kept pulsing around him.

My hair stuck to his wet chest, my ribcage pushing hard against him as I struggled for breath. He rocked me up and down. I closed my eyes and almost drifted away, lulled into darkness by a sense of satisfaction even deeper than I'd felt before. I moaned and stretched on top of him like a kitten, and he chuckled.

His arms fell on me out of nowhere, squeezed me tight against his chest. I jumped off him and the bed as if burned, wheezing as I struggled to breathe. I found myself pushing into the wall opposite him, eyes wide and limbs trembling. He just stood there on the bed, mouth hanging open and worry drowning the soft glow in his eyes.

"Beatrice? What's wrong?"

I shook my head, held up my hands in despair as he made to crawl to the end of the bed.

"Stay there," I managed to say between wheezes.

His brows furrowed, and I could feel him itching to move closer. It only served to make my freak-out worse, the lingering thoughts of us together making everything more intense. I bit hard on the inside of my cheek and focused on that pain, on the sting of it. Why had I risked it? I wasn't stupid enough to think it would end well, and yet there I was making a fool of myself on his floor. I shot to my feet and ran into the guest bedroom, closing the door behind me and leaning against it, sliding down to the floor.

It took him little time to come knocking, of course. His house, but he was knocking on the door and that made me laugh in a mangled, breathless sort of way.

"Bea, you okay? Please open the door."

"Go away."

He sighed and thumped harder against the door. He could have pushed in, pushed on the knob. But he didn't—he just kept demanding that I let him in. That was what scared me about the whole situation, I realized bitterly. That was what truly terrified me right then—the fact he could not push in but demanded I let him in. And I'd been making small concessions as we were in the heat of passion, so it wasn't that much of a thing for him to close his arms around me earlier. It stung that he hadn't done anything wrong, but I was punishing him for it. Punishing myself for allowing him to get that close in the first place. I leaned my head back against the door and tears flooded down my face. This was why I hated Richie turning violent on me. This would never have happened with him. Not even him pushing me face-down into the bed didn't cause me to freak out as badly.

"I'm not going anywhere, Bea. You'll have to come out of there at some point."

I didn't trust myself to speak. Instead, I bit harder into my cheek and allowed the tears to run down my face. I'd open that door when everything was all done and over with. Maybe he'd fall asleep waiting, and I could crawl out and just…I didn't know what. Go back home? So what if Sam would try to kick my ass? I'd handle that somehow. I had no issue with introducing him to my baseball bat, after all. I wasn't afraid of Sam, and maybe that was part of my problem. If he came at me with clear intention to hurt me, I could easily swing that bat at his head. No problem there. Anthony trying to hug me, on the other hand? Major freak-out material.

Tears stopped rolling down, and I gave my face a while to get back into moderately human shape. When I opened the door, Anthony was standing there, butt naked. He was worried, but also annoyed. Those eyes of his were so strong and expressive I most likely could've read him from across a football field.

"We need to talk," I croaked out.

One of his eyebrows went up. "You think?"

I crossed my arms over my chest. Being naked was suddenly embarrassing. Too intimate, like this was more than just getting off together. Like I was opening another door, not just the one of his guest bedroom. I stepped back inside and took the cover off the bed to wrap around myself. He just stood there, watching me with a mix of amusement and sadness.

"In case it escaped your notice, I saw you naked already."

I clutched the cover tighter around me and sat on the bed.

"But you need to put layers between us now, huh?" He smiled as he spoke without a trace of humor in his eyes. "I'm sorry I…tried to hug you. Obviously, I had no idea it would be this traumatic."

"This is all my fault, Anthony. I'm sorry. Really sorry. I'll get my things and—"

"You'll keep your plump little ass right where it is. You'll look up from the goddamn floor, acknowledge there's another human being in the room who you've accidentally been making love to for the past hour, and tell me what's going on."

My shoulders slumped. He was pissed. Of course he was. This made no sense. I made no sense. I inhaled deeply and looked at him. He was so intense right then that I had to swallow a few times just to manage speaking. Which, in light of everything that had happened between us, was ridiculous. I was ridiculous, and well aware of it. I just had to do him the courtesy of making him aware, too.

"I have…issues with being held down. I don't mean that in an abstract sort of way, though I guess it applies even there. I mean, I freak out if you overpower me. Even the slightest. Scares the hell out of me. I would probably try to kill you if you climbed on top of me right now, for instance."

He remained silent for a while. A lot of different emotions played through his eyes, many of them almost choking me. He inhaled deeply and blew out the air, then breathed in again more calmly.

"How long has this been going on?"

Ah, not the direct question then. He was a smart guy, on top of everything else. I was in so much trouble.

"Two years," I answered as calmly as I could.

"Okay, what happened two years ago?"

There it was, the big question.

Chapter 8

Secrets are living things that eat at your soul. You keep them hidden because you're afraid everyone will know not what you're hiding, but how much of you your secrets have been eating. How little you've been able to fight their monstrous hunger. My father used to tell me that all the time. Of course, to him it was a good way to make sure he knew everything about my mom and me. There were no secrets among us, so we were strong—or so he said. At least my mom and I were strong; I think he always had at least one terrible, terrible secret. Maybe it was that secret that ate at him until there was no soul left. Maybe he spoke from experience when he told us about how secrets mangled the soul.

My stomach roiled each time I thought about him. If I searched my heart, I had to admit it wasn't what he'd done that shamed me—it hadn't been my fault. What shamed me was how I couldn't stand to be hugged or focused on too intensely by someone now. What shamed me was how little I trusted myself to move somehow beyond that secret. How it spread dark tentacles and overtook everything about my life, about my heart.

I looked back into Anthony's eyes. Did he have secrets? Was he ashamed of how they crippled his soul? This man I'd known only for one day had shaken me and my life worse than anything else in the last two years. Maybe it wasn't a good idea to give him any more than I already had. Maybe it wasn't fair to burden him any more than I already had.

"Bea?"

He crawled to me on his knees, naked. I wish I could say I didn't notice his bare butt because of the nature of the moment, only I did notice it. It made me chuckle, a light, airy sound that floated above us. He reached my knees and sat back on his haunches, dark eyes turbulent enough to consume me. Air whooshed out of my lungs as I held his gaze. This was beyond chemistry, something between a curse and a blessing. It tingled and burned through me, stirred up everything from the deepest pit of my soul. My skin burst out in goose bumps, and I reached out and touched his face. The stubble grazed my palm, and yet it was the sweetest, softest touch I'd ever felt.

"I wish I could be…better. I wish I could be normal, you know? A whole soul. But I don't feel like I am."

He frowned. "You are a whole soul. Bea, whatever it is, we'll work through it. I've never been as crazy about someone as quickly as I am about you. Don't push me away. Don't run from this. From us. When I touch you, it's like my soul shivers with joy, like every part of my body is a focus point of pleasure. You feel the same, don't you?"

I gulped and just stared.

"Tell me you feel the same," he whispered.

I couldn't say it, but I nodded. He reached out and took my foot, placed it on his thigh. Then he did the same with the other one. Anthony Gowl was a silly man, and I loved that about him. It took courage to be silly in the face of a crippled soul. I admired his courage.

"Tell you what," he said, smiling. "Don't tell me what bothers you so much. If it makes it easier, we'll never mention this again. Just tell me exactly what to do so I don't take you there again. How about that?"

I shrugged. "I'll tell you. At some point, when it'll make no difference between us. I'll tell you then."

"Okay," he said, massaging my feet. "It's a deal. Now help me steer clear of it."

"It's not one certain thing—that's what sucks about this. It can be just the way you look at me and the way I react to it, like it was in your office last night. I don't deal well with hugging, because you're so big and strong and I like it, but when you hug me or loom over me it…takes me there."

"Okay, so no hugging, no looming. I'm not sure about the looking at you thing. I mean, I can not loom or not hug, but the way I look at you…"

I reached out and caressed his lips with my fingers. "I think we worked out the looking thing. I'm sorry, hugging is a big no-no. Though I really wish you could hug me, that I could take it and love the comfort and…"

He shook his head. "Maybe we'll get there. But in the meantime, no looming or hugging. Got it. Anything else?"

"No going daddy-mode on me. No keeping things from me thinking I can't handle them, no making decisions for me. Don't try to be my hero. I don't need or want one. I couldn't stand one."

He looked stricken for a moment. "Yeah, that might be a bit… difficult. I tend to go…daddy-mode. Especially with people I care about."

"Then don't care about me."

"I think that train has pretty much left the station, Bea."

He smiled and I smiled back, lost. What the hell was I doing here? What was he doing? It made no sense. But then again, the best things in life made no sense. Curling your toes when you had a cup of your favorite coffee didn't make sense, but it was beyond beautiful. Crying when watching a movie made no sense, but it eased your soul and made you feel alive. Though the simple fact you're breathing makes you alive, it's always things that make your heart shudder that make you *feel* alive. Does that make any sense? So I liked the fact we made no sense. It meant it was one of those things we'd remember fondly for the rest of our lives, even if we ended up in a world of hurt.

I got one of my bright ideas and grinned. "Can I ask you something?"

He nodded.

"Would you please climb in bed and lie down? Just lie down."

He smiled. "Doesn't sound like a big effort."

He got up on the bed and lay down beside me. I focused on my breathing for a while, turned to look at him, and clutched the covers I wore. "Now stand very, very still. Okay?"

He nodded again, curiosity and amusement radiating from his eyes. I crawled slowly toward him, keeping the cover in place. I felt too naked right then to drop it, childish as it was. I plastered myself on him and rested my head on his chest. His heart beat strongly, and his smell danced down my throat to feed that starving part of me. I breathed out shakily with relief and allowed every muscle in my body to relax.

"I won't be able to sleep beside you," I whispered. "It's one of those sure things that freak me out. But I'd love to stay like this for a bit. Can we do that?"

"Sure, sparrow."

"Why 'sparrow'?"

He laughed softly. "You remind me of this bird my sister used to have when we were kids. She wasn't a pet store bird, just some small lively thing she'd somehow managed to find. That bird spent time in her room, fluttered around. Meli built it a nest on her nightstand. On her birthday that year I bought her a birdcage. It made sense to me to get her a home for the bird, you know? So I gave her that birdcage. She put it on a table in her room, tried to introduce the bird to it. But that bird took one look at it, fluttered its wings, and flew away. I don't even remember why the window was open, but it shot out through it. Never came back. Maybe it died out there, who knows? But Meli slept with her windows open for a full year, refused to let us close them. Each time we'd try to close them she'd get this puppy-eyed look and say, 'What if Sparrow wants to come home and the windows are closed?'"

He was silent for a while. I saw where the similarity came from. But something else clicked into place, too. Sparrow had flown away from his sister and never came back. I didn't mention that. Instead, I lifted my head to look at him. "So you have a sister?"

His eyes lost all light, total desolation washing through him. "I had a sister. Meli's been gone for seven years. Cocaine addiction… she didn't make it."

Cold shivers crawled through my spine. "I'm so sorry."

He smiled that little, humorless smile of his. "Not as sorry as I am. I should've tried harder to break her vicious circle. But I was stupid enough to think she'd protect herself at some point."

I thought of my mom, of the sick relationship she had with my father. Back when they were young, her parents had been stupid enough to think she'd protect herself from him, too. She hadn't. Maybe she couldn't—whatever tied them together was stronger than she was. Addictions to people were worse than those to drugs as far as I was concerned. At least drugs looked like poison. People who were poison didn't look like it, though. They looked just like everybody else, and by the time you realized they were poison it was too late.

"Sometimes you can't save people from themselves. They don't want to be saved, sometimes. They refuse to be," I whispered.

We lay there in silence for maybe a couple of hours. Until he began to move.

"Think it's time to get ready for work, hmm?"

I got up, still clutching the covers around my body. The freak out had been safely averted, but I did need those extra layers between us. He stood beside me and leaned down to kiss the bridge of my nose. My heart fluttered and I smiled.

"I'll get your bag up here, okay? Shower, change, get your stuff done, and when you're ready to go, knock on my door."

I stared at him as he turned around to leave. If this had been a movie or a book, I'd call his name and ask him to hug me, to kiss me, to love me. I'd probably ask him to stay or say something poignant, something that would mark our future together.

"Anthony?"

"Yeah?" he called over his shoulder.

"Thanks."

"I told you already, sparrow. Whatever I can do for you, it's my pleasure."

Then he walked out, closing the door behind him. Was that maybe the scene to predict the end of this story? Him walking out, back turned to me and to what had happened? It didn't feel like a satisfying ending. I didn't want it. And yet other versions still terrified me. Fear and desire, Anthony's flavor. I touched the bridge of my nose, ran the tips of my fingers over it. The skin tingled where he'd kissed it. I smiled like a kid and ignored the bad feeling that wrapped around my gut. Whatever future would come, right now I was his sparrow. Maybe that meant he wouldn't try to cage me in so I wouldn't fly away. Maybe the ending wouldn't matter. All that mattered was that right now my skin tingled where he'd kissed it.

I thought about his sister as I took a long, cleansing shower. Had she worn her addiction with pride? Or had it drained her of her soul, eaten her from the inside out? I thought about my mother and the black splotches she sometimes wore like badges of honor. It was beyond me how anyone could claim to love someone else but then hurt them so bluntly time and time again. How could they live with themselves knowing what they'd done?

Then again, some couldn't—my father obviously couldn't live with it in the end. But it didn't stop him from hurting her, from killing her. Maybe it was because part of being alive meant being cruel. So those like my father were the honest ones, perhaps. They wore their cruelty close to the skin, made it easy to see for everyone who cared enough to look. But then why hadn't anyone seen the extent of that cruelty before it was too late? Why hadn't I? The rational side of me kept repeating it wasn't my fault, none of it. That I couldn't have predicted such a monstrous end to my parents' story; not even in my darkest nightmares could I have imagined he'd viciously murder her. But maybe if I'd said something about the bruises I saw all those years, maybe if I'd asked her to leave him, to save herself…Maybe I'd be able to see her golden eyes crinkle at the corners while she laughed. God, how I missed her.

At least those guys in the Playroom were honest and open about their pleasures. They terrified me on a deeper level than I was willing to ponder, but I respected their honesty. They stopped when asked to—at least most of them did. The ones who didn't got thrown out by Doug or someone like him. They didn't push the pain beyond what someone else was willing—no, eager—to take. Had my mother and father been closet cases of the same thing? Had Anthony's sister and her drug? Maybe some weren't strong enough to admit they thrived on someone else's pain knowing they'd been the ones to inflict it. And the secret of what they enjoyed ate at their souls, like my father used to say. The more they denied their nature the worse it ate at them, until there was nothing at all left. No soul, no human heart. They were walking, talking, breathing shells. So it made sense that they sucked out the souls of those around them. Didn't we all try to fill the holes in our souls? They were just better at it and had bigger holes to fill.

I stared at my eyes in the mirror as I put on my dark makeup. Mom's laughter echoed around the bathroom for one heart-shattering moment. She used to laugh so much when we were alone together. I couldn't remember her laughing around my father. Maybe he was so miserable he sucked the fun right out of her. Fed on it to keep breathing. Had she been afraid of him?

Had she been terrified? Had no one seen she lived in terror, if she had? Had no one tried to help? But maybe nobody saw. Nobody knew. I didn't truly understand the degree of danger she embraced every day, not until it was too late. She was so brave, my mother. Foolish, perhaps, but brave. It took guts to sleep and eat and live with a monster, hoping he wouldn't turn on you. But then again, she probably didn't see him as a monster. Anthony's sister hadn't seen her drug as a monster either, most likely. Not until it was too late. Not until there was no salvation within reach.

A tear slid down my cheek, muddying my face. The mirror had fogged up, and all I could see was a vague contour of a woman. A nameless creature with one dark streak of makeup running down her face. A sparrow that ran in fear of everything looking remotely like a cage. Because this sparrow knew how viciously those walls could close around it, how they could poke into its heart and bleed it dry.

I was a coward, but running meant I'd be alive. I didn't have to be brave like my mother. I didn't need the badges of honor to say I'd fought and stood my ground, that I'd risked. No. I was okay with running away. It seemed like the smaller crime. In the back of my mind, I knew running would not only keep me going, but also save everyone else from the monster inside me. Because I'd lost chunks of my soul too, and did it really matter where or when or how? They weren't there anymore. I'd need to fill that void, so I'd prey on someone or something to rebuild myself. Just like my father, I might end up draining the life out of those who stood too close. Running was the best thing I could do for everyone. And yet right now I didn't feel like running. I was too exhausted to even walk. I wanted to stop for a while, just a short while.

I wiped away the steam on the mirror with trembling hands. I cleaned the ruined makeup and redid it. Better. Much better. I closed my eyes and went back into how yesterday night had felt while I was dancing. I allowed the craving of all those watching to fill me. When I opened my eyes they looked filled to the brim again. I was a full person, a full soul. When I danced, I took what others had to spare to fill that void in my heart. And it made me proud that I could do it. That I wasn't an empty monster sucking the life out of those closest to me. I just took their leftovers in the middle of the night and glued them together into the shape of a full heart. If I danced more, maybe I could stop running just for a short while.

When I was all set to go, I knocked on his bedroom door. It opened to reveal the best-looking man I'd ever seen. He wore a black suit with a black shirt underneath and a crimson necktie.

"Oh, my God," I said hoarsely. "I wanna lick you all over."

He chuckled and tucked one hand in his pocket. "Exactly what I was thinking. I wanna lick you all over…again."

I blushed and looked into his eyes. "Is Doug coming?"

He shook his head and smiled that humorless smile of his. "He's staying with Tina. Let's go."

We would've been such a good fit if I'd been wearing my dancing costume right then. But I would be wearing it shortly.

When we got to the club, I looked around, a bit disoriented.

"We're going through the front entrance," he said, reaching out a hand.

Oh-key…so we were making the Entrance, holding hands. Okey-dokey, then. Never mind that I was blushing like some schoolgirl and annoyed at the situation for God only knew what reason. He took my hand in his and rubbed his thumb against my wrist as we walked in. A bouncer wearing a black suit smiled and opened the door.

"Evening, boss."

"Everything all right, James?"

The guy nodded, not even glancing in my direction. Was that a comment on me or on Anthony? I couldn't decide. I also couldn't decide which would annoy me more.

"If anything funny happens you let me know, yes?"

"Yes, sir. But I'm sure things will go just fine. They always do."

The main doors, big, heavy double ones like the ones at the entrance of the Playroom, led into a sort of receiving area. A hostess stood primly behind her glossy black desk, hair perfectly coiffed and black shirt—or dress, I couldn't see behind that desk—showing generous cleavage. Her lips were small and bright red, long black lashes blinking at us. Coming in here to see that would make someone a regular pretty easy, I guessed. Everything about the place said Anthony and Justine were pretty smart business people. That would mean they had great instincts. I had a healthy amount of respect for good instincts—one of those things I wished I had.

There was also a wardrobe, complete with a chick in a simple, skin-tight black dress. She was surreally beautiful, but unlike the hostess she looked like a natural beauty. Not a perfect nose, not the perfect sized, puffy lips, just good proportions and gorgeous eyes. All backed up by mountains of confidence and a heap of charm. She reminded me a bit of Justine. I sighed as the memory of her beautiful face shot through my mind. How badly had she been beaten? Was her face…affected? I shuddered as the wardrobe chick inspected me with entirely too much focus.

She smiled and titled her head to the side a bit. "You're the new dancer, am I right?"

I nodded as Anthony talked to the hostess chick. The woman quirked her perfect lips, and her eyes flashed with something not quite kind. Ah, so she was one of those who wanted Anthony. I was public enemy number one, sweeping in to take the jackpot she'd been trying to get for who knew how long.

"Yeah, I'm Beatrice."

Wardrobe girl smiled wider and reached out a hand. "Sarah. But you shouldn't use your real name here. You should have a stage name, you know? You're the main attraction of Satine so you should go for something…deliciously sexy. Just like you."

Anthony chose that moment to pay attention, and he grinned. "Don't hit on my girlfriend, Sarah."

She pouted. "That's cruel, boss. You didn't even give the rest of us a chance, snatched her up first day."

"What can I say, I couldn't resist."

Sarah giggled. "I entirely understand your point. Saw her dance last night. Hot stuff."

"I know, right?"

I rolled my eyes. "I'm standing right here, guys. Stop talking like I'm invisible. Is Sarah right? Should I have a stage name or something?"

"Hmm…Yeah, guess so. The main dancer would be introduced with all the pomp of being our star. Definitely need a stage name. Had one before?"

I shook my head. "Didn't really need one."

"Everyone has an alter ego here," Sarah said, leaning on the counter. "How about…Delice?"

Anthony snorted. "Doesn't fit. Maybe—"

"Varana," I blurted out. "I'll be Varana."

Sarah nodded, seemingly delighted. Anthony watched me closely, trying to find something in my eyes. Good instincts. But he couldn't find anything there; my eyes were aimed at anything else but at him. Finally he broke down and asked. "Why that particular name? Just thought it up or…?"

"My mom's maiden name."

I left it at that, so he nodded and we went inside. The Playroom stood to our right at the end of the dark hallway, the Satine to our left and in the middle the lush lounge area with those spectacular booths. Something of a crossroads, I thought. The place was beautiful—it had a great overall vibe. Well, maybe except the scary one from the room on the right. But I was anxious to get inside

Satine and on my cube. There was my freedom, my salvation. The one I could rely on, the one that never failed to deliver.

As soon as we got through Satine's doors, the crowd invaded my senses. It felt like more people had shown up tonight; the place almost shook with everyone's energy. I couldn't wait to play to it, to feed on it. Anthony took me to his office and closed the door behind him, grinning.

"Could I please help you put that costume on?"

I *tsked*. "Not very proper of you to ask, Mr. Gowl."

"Who said I was proper?"

I turned around and set the bag down. "You can't help me." Looking over my shoulder, though, I added, "But you can watch."

He laughed gruffly. "You're determined to give me a stroke."

"Not at all, Mr. Gowl. You're determined to give yourself one, it seems."

Not turning around, I did my best to move as lasciviously as possible getting my gear on. I heard him breathing harder over there by the door but I was determined to keep going. When I was all ready, I finally turned around and smiled. He looked like he needed me right then. I loved that glow on his face.

"I'm thirty, and when I look at you it's like I'm a teenager."

I smiled. "Thirty? Really?"

"Too much of a grownup for you, sparrow?"

I stuck my tongue out at him and fixed my gloves up. "Depends," I said, not looking up. "If you start showing signs of Saggy Butt Syndrome soon, I might run screaming."

He snorted. "Fear not, lover. My butt is gonna stay nice and firm."

"Then we're all right," I said and grinned.

Chapter 9

We went out to the DJ's station as soon as we returned to Satine. Anthony kept a hand on the small of my back, not pushing but keeping close to my every step. I tried to shake him off twice, discreetly of course. He feigned not noticing, not so discreetly grinning at me. Daddy was part of his genetic makeup or something. At the moment it was a small offense though, and I wasn't freaking out over it so I made the small concession. Hopefully he'd work out some of those clingy needs that way, and I wouldn't run into monster manifestations of it…like hugging me.

As we walked by, a young couple kissed and hugged. I didn't turn my head, walked as if I hadn't even noticed their existence. But I stared out of the corner of my eye. I envied them for the ease with which they touched, for her smooth glide into his arms. I wondered what each of them felt when they embraced. What did a normal, full-soul person feel when hugging or being hugged? It had been at least two years since I'd last been hugged. Honestly, I didn't remember much about it. I hadn't been overly touchy-feely back then either, but now I regretted not paying more attention to each hug. It was small things like that I took for granted back then: being hugged, making out with a boyfriend without going insane because he'd climbed on top of me, coming home to talk to my mom about whatever. God, how I missed talking to her. And the soft crinkles around her eyes and lips when she smiled. Small things really hurt worse than the big, dramatic ones. Everything reminded me of the small things.

"This is Chris," Anthony hollered in my ear.

I nodded at the DJ and shook his hand. The guy smiled, nodded as Anthony told him something.

"So what should I play for your dancing pleasure?" Chris asked.

It very tempting to roll my eyes at him, but I didn't. "I loved the beats last night. Just none of that throbby house stuff. I'm not a fan."

The man nodded gravely. Yeah, he wasn't a fan either. Fabulous. The frequency of my headaches would drop dramatically. Anthony snuck a hand up my spine. Well, maybe the headaches wouldn't disappear entirely. I made to turn around and face the cube, and Chris grabbed the mic and grinned at me widely.

"And, the lady we've all been waiting for, Varanaaaa!"

Christ, what was this, a boxing match? I pinched the bridge of my nose under the tilted hat and walked up the stairs to my cube. *Men.* A few of the ones hanging around the cube actually clapped, looking all excited. I recognized them from last night, so I smiled and took an ornate bow. A seductive beat began throbbing though the room, and I assumed my starting position. I threw my body into the beat and ate up all the attention I got, gave it back to them each with smiles and winks and extra sways of my hips.

There was a sitting area with tables on the half-floor ahead of me. Right at the center table I could make out a familiar face, so I tipped my hat to him and he waved. Colorful lasers threw strange shadows around, but I could make out his face easily. He was one of my high-roller fans, the one who'd sent me the Cristal each night at the Pearl. How had they already found out I was here? Just one night and he already knew. How fast did news travel?

Anthony didn't hover around as I danced. I really appreciated that. I noticed a waiter carry the bottle of Cristal to Chris, and a familiar song filled the Satine. The one my top fan always managed to extract from the DJ at the Pearl. I did my usual routine to it for him, my thank you for his loyalty. Chris sipped at the Cristal with gusto, his reward for playing ball, I presumed. Where would my usual bottle go now? To Anthony's office? That was certainly going to be interesting.

Hours flew by as I worked out my demons on the cube. My muscles tingled pleasantly and burned with the effort by the time the crowd thinned out again. I did my ornate bow when I was done and found the Cristal at the bottom of the stairs to the cube. Chris got out of his booth and leaned in to whisper. I casually stepped just a bit back. He wasn't as tall as Anthony or Doug, but I felt like he was looming over me. He kept the smile on but allowed me the space, screaming louder to make sure the words got across.

"This is the first complimentary Cristal I ever got for one song. You have seriously hardcore admirers, huh?"

I shrugged. "Just one of those. I don't even know his name."

He shook his head, laughed, and clinked his Cristal against mine.

"I might get used to this kinna treatment," he shouted after taking a swig.

I sort of had, I guess. I grinned back and looked around for Anthony. I'd expected him to be here. But he wasn't, so I just walked into his office determined to change and massage my feet a little. Those high heels were biting into my feet. It would take a bit more time to get used to dancing on them for a few hours. They clicked sexily against the pristine white floors of Anthony's office, though. Each time I looked down at them, I remembered him inside me and shivered a bit. Honestly, I was looking forward to getting him alone again. Especially after dancing. I felt frisky. As if summoned, he showed up, closed the door behind him, and locked it.

I turned around. "Where—"

Words stuck in my throat. The person standing there and leaning back against the locked door wasn't Anthony at all.

"Varana," the man said, grinning. "I've been meaning to introduce myself. Just never got around to it at the Pearl. I'm happy you gave me the chance tonight."

My chest tightened in fear but I tried to keep a brave front. There had been no chance given. The man had just taken the opportunity to follow me through that *Employees Only* sign. It was probably too subtle, all bold and red as it was. I forced my lips into a tight smile.

"You have me at a disadvantage here. You know my name, but I don't know yours."

"Sorry, how rude. I'm Marcus Forder, and I'm entirely delighted to finally meet you."

He strutted up to me and stuck his hand out. I took deep, even breaths. *Relax, Beatrice, you can do this*. I slowly put my hand in his. To my utter horror, he lifted it up to his lips and trailed a few kisses all the way up to my wrist. Cold shivers traveled through my bones, eardrums pounding. Where was Anthony? I swallowed thickly.

"How did you know I was here at the Satine?"

He pouted. "I'm a resourceful man, Varana. I would've found you in another state, let alone in the same town."

Entirely not like a stalker, I thought. Admirers were a great thing to have, as long as they didn't encroach on your private space. Up close and personal, he gave me a bit of a tight tummy. My lips began to tremble as I kept up the fake smile. He'd called me Varana though, which meant he didn't know my real name, right? Or maybe he was just using the one I'd used as courtesy to my dancing persona. But if he knew I was here, he had to know more about me. That unsettled the hell out of me. Maybe someone at the Pearl had told him more about me. Sam wouldn't have sent a high-roller out to a new club risking he'd become a regular here.

"Please, sit down," I gritted out.

He sat in one of the twin black chairs in front of Anthony's desk, so I hurried to sit in the boss chair. I liked that distance between us; the desk itself brought me comfort. Maybe because the place smelled like Anthony, too, but a girl had to take comfort in whatever she could at times like these.

"So, Mr. Forder, thank you for the Cristal."

He smiled. "Marcus, please. Entirely my pleasure. I'd like to do more for your enjoyment, in fact."

Terrible greed flashed through his eyes, and my skin prickled up. "Like what?"

"Anything you'd allow me to do, Varana. Anything at all. A trip around the world in my private jet, a cruise on my yacht, shopping around Europe. Whatever you feel like."

I blinked a few times, stunned. The guy must've been filthy rich. The Cristal had been clue enough, I guess, but throwing in a private jet, a yacht, and topping it with shopping around Europe went beyond some imaginary line of the possible. It didn't sit right. Wealth looked suspicious to me. I couldn't help it. We'd been piss-poor as I grew up, and I was poor on my own. Anthony was much better off than me, and it bothered me on a level I couldn't appease, but this guy? This guy was filthy rich. He seemed to come from an entirely different universe or might as well have. Flashing all his goods like I'd be blinded by their blingy-bling and throw myself at his feet wasn't as seductive as he might have hoped. I found it annoying, in fact. But I had been taking his Cristal and selling them to a friend. The money had come in handy, and now I had to pay the price for taking those bottles. It was what I'd always feared, but since he'd never made a move to go further than watching me dance, I'd taken it for granted he wouldn't.

"If I may ask, why haven't you approached me before? Why only now?"

He took it entirely the wrong way, became all lecherous. "You should've approached me, lovely. I didn't know if you were interested, and Sam kept threatening to ban me from his club if I made a move."

Of course he would. If the rich guy scratched his itch, he might not come back and splurge at the Pearl every night I was there. I smiled as coldly as I could. "I'm not available, Marcus."

"It's the owner here, isn't it? I saw him hovering around you. I can give you *so* much more, Varana."

He looked at me in such a way that for one terrifying second he reminded me of my father, of the way he looked at my mom. It was that owner-like stare that freaked me out entirely. His eyes said I'd be one of his decorative objects, another private jet or yacht, something to use at will. Christ, the man had no reason to remind me of my father. None at all. But he did. Maybe because I was so frazzled about what was going on with Anthony, memories stirred and attacked me. My insides clenched painfully, and cold sweat bloomed over my body. His brows furrowed.

"Are you okay?"

I nodded. "Just tired. Thanks for the offer, but I'm okay with what I have now."

He reached out a card, pushed it across the desk as close to me as it would go. It fit his style, all fancy and tastefully done. It had his personal contacts on the back written in fine lettering. There were some things money did buy, just not me.

"I'm a patient man, lovely. I'll wait for you to call me when you're ready to have everything you deserve."

Charming. Marcus Forder struck me as the kind of man who got things done. Maybe all his attention shouldn't go entirely to waste.

"I could use your help with something…delicate," I said, looking up into his steely-blue eyes.

They lit up. "My pleasure. Whatever I can do."

"You know who owns this place?"

"Of course, Anthony Gowl and Justine Sanders. Why?"

I bit my lip. "Justine was attacked last night. Know anything about that?"

His eyes turned speculative, and he leaned back a little. "Why would I?"

I didn't want him on the defensive. So I turned the smile warmer. "Maybe Sam mentioned something, if you talked to him."

His gaze turned calculating as he crossed his legs. There was an angle to work here. I was sure he'd be smart enough to notice it. Getting me all grateful might be in his favor. I could practically see his face change as he latched on to that possibility.

"Sam had her beaten up because Satine stole you? Well, I never would've suspected Sam of too much class, so I'm not surprised. Between you and me, this is a far better place to work."

I thought the same. "He threatened me too."

"Did he now?"

"So I hear. But I didn't peg him for a girl-beater. Then again, he had a suspiciously transparent, twisted reason—taking revenge. So I'm wondering if he's stooped that low, if he'd do it again. Do you think he would?"

"I'm very happy you brought this up, lovely. It'll be a pleasure for me to make sure he won't harm you."

I fluttered my lashes, smiled coyly. "Oh, I didn't mean it like that. Just wondered if you think he's capable of it."

But he had made up his mind already. I felt a tug of guilt for it, but if he was determined to do something for me this was way more useful than drowning me in Cristal.

I knew men like Marcus. They had the daddy vibe and got frustrated if there was nothing to act it out on. If he wanted to act like my daddy, he could work it out with Sam. That would mean Anthony would have less space to go all daddy-mode on me, hopefully. It would make everyone a little happier. I didn't really care about Marcus, so he wasn't in danger of getting close to me. But Anthony had crawled right under my skin already, and I needed to put some distance there. Enough to be able to hang around him for a while, at least. I leaned back in his chair, hated the way my heart fluttered each time a gust of his smell flew up around me. Why couldn't I just have one thing easy? One goddamn thing, was it that much to ask for?

The office door opened and Anthony walked in, frowning. "Funny thing is, this is my office and yet I didn't know I was having a meeting with anyone."

Marcus grinned but didn't turn around. "Evening, Mr. Gowl. Varana and I were just chatting. We're old friends."

"Are you?"

Anthony's dark eyes bored into me. I pushed harder into the back of the chair but smiled.

"Marcus used to hang out with me at the Pearl. He's going to hang out at the Satine now, huh?"

He grinned and nodded. "Much better company here. Plus the place is way classier, so congrats on getting the classiest dancer for it, Mr. Gowl."

Anthony stuck both hands into his pockets and sat down in the chair next to Marcus. "I just got lucky, really. It was Justine who managed that."

"Yes, I'm sorry about your associate. Varana was just telling me about the incident. It's a crying shame anyone would raise a hand to a woman."

Dark eyes flashed at me again—angry or just anxious, I couldn't tell. I kept my face carefully composed, crossed my legs in his chair and massaged the armrests. I nursed a sliver of guilt about taking the Cristal, but I hoped Anthony wouldn't take it as guilt about something else.

Marcus cleared his throat, got up, and reached out to shake Anthony's hand. Of course Anthony got up and shook it, smiled like they were business partners, not two guys competing for my dubious attention.

"Marcus Forder."

"Glad to meet you, Mr. Forder. Hope we'll see you around the Satine."

"Oh, you will. You can bet on that. I'll take my leave now. I'm sure Varana is tired. Good night."

"Night," I muttered.

He closed his suit jacket and walked out in style. Marcus Forder was a handsome man, wealthy and powerful. You could read that in the way he walked—that level of confidence didn't come without a level of achievement. I liked thinking I had someone like that to call in case of need. Anthony would burst a vein if he knew that, but there was no reason for him to. I turned to look at him as he sat back down in the chair.

"I know Forder sent you and Chris each Cristal. That's the kind of thing that someone notices easily. Cristal isn't all that subtle, is it? So what's up with him?"

I shrugged. "Don't push, Anthony. He's one of my…regular admirers back at the Pearl. He's been sending me a bottle of Cristal every night for months."

He snorted. "What the hell do you do, bathe in the stuff?"

I chuckled. "Sell it, to be honest. I don't drink anything fancier than beer."

He sighed, propped his elbow on the armrest and his chin on his hand. "He's very into you. I can see it a mile away."

"And?"

His lips tightened and he averted his gaze. "And you shouldn't play around with men like that. He could turn aggressive. He's obviously infatuated with you."

"And you're not? Anything beyond a passing fancy is infatuation, isn't it?"

"I'm your…lover."

"Are you? Wanted to say 'boyfriend,' didn't you? You failed to ask me how I'd feel about that before mentioning it to Sarah earlier."

He looked back at me, eyes speculative. "Should I have said I'm your temporary squeeze? Would that sound better?"

I sighed. "Jealousy doesn't go well with your suit."

He chuckled, got up from the chair, and bent over the desk. His eyes stalked all over my body; I felt his desire brushing all over me. My hands tightened on the armrests as he loomed there. My pulse spiked. But my breathing didn't go shallower because of a freak out. It did because I remembered the way his tongue felt on me.

"I want to make love to you on this desk, Bea."

My throat tightened. "That's something I can't give you."

I got up slowly, ran a hand over the ruffles of my boxers. Looking up into his eyes, I licked my lips and loved the way his jaw slackened. Something shifted between us, and the buzz became heavy, thick. Air grew sticky as it slid into my lungs.

"Sit down on the rug." I spoke as evenly as I could.

He did as told and my heart fluttered. I walked up to him with an extra sway to my hips. The view of his strong body sprawled there at my feet made me throb inside. I nibbled on my lips and ran a hand down between my legs, squishing ruffles as I went. His pants began to tent deliciously.

"Get yourself out," I whispered thickly.

He worked quickly, holding his hard length in one hand.

"Don't touch yourself. You're mine to touch."

His gaze burned up, called to me like a siren. My body responded to him, welled up with want. He was painfully deep under my skin already; it scared the hell out of me. And yet I found it oddly erotic too.

"Hands behind your head and hold them there."

He quickly did as told. After taking one glove off, I went to my knees and crawled over him until I reached my target. It jumped up at me, burning hot and smooth to the touch. His hips flexed as I stroked him, lips parted in a sigh of pleasure as I slowly licked my palm before grabbing him and tugging at his hard length with my wet palm.

"Now keep very, very still for me…"

I opened my lips on him, and he slowly slid into my mouth. His taste exploded on the tip of my tongue as I lapped at him, stroked the underside of him while my lips tightened around his girth. He groaned and I sucked him harder, hungrier. He whined adorably as I slid up his length and let him drop against his pants.

"This is what I can give you, Anthony. Is it enough?"

"I want more."

I chuckled and rubbed my gloved fingers against his plump tip. He hissed, hips flexing softly under my touch. "But you won't try to take more. You'll just receive what I have to give. Won't you?"

He whimpered as I scraped my teeth around his head. I loved the way he purred beneath my hands, loved the need oozing from his pores. It went through my body like lightning and scorched my insides. It made my panties grow damp. Having him to tease, to play with, to enjoy—it felt wonderful, intoxicating.

"Someone could come in. The door isn't locked," I whispered.

His eyes shot open at me, but I made sure to push my palm against his hips and tug at his length.

"They'd see you here at my mercy, straining hard and yet so pliant."

I sucked him down my throat, swallowed around him. He groaned, muscles going solid as stone under my hands. He mumbled something, frustrated as I dropped him from my mouth again.

"Did you say something?"

Dark eyes flashed open at me, bottomless and scorching hot. "Please, Bea."

"What do you want? Tell me. Ask for it like a good boy…"

My gloved hand snuck up his stomach and chest, and I pinched one of his nipples through the smooth fabric of his shirt.

He shuddered as I gripped his base and poked at his slit with my fingertip.

"Suck me off."

I chuckled. "You didn't say 'pretty please,' baby. Say it."

"Pretty please," he said gruffly.

I licked around his head, lapped at the clear drops at his tip. "Again," I spoke right into his hot head.

He sucked in a deep breath, biceps flexing. God, he was so beautiful. And mine, at least right now. I could have him for right now—it was all that mattered. All that I cared about.

"Please…" he rasped as I gripped him harder.

I took him in deeply, hummed around his length, and ate him up with hunger. His thighs tensed up, and I sucked him harder, deeper, swallowed around him and kept humming, moaning with him deeply lodged inside my throat. As he came, I swallowed and moaned harder until his hips shivered. When he was done, I licked him all over once again, loving the way he twitched.

"You're delicious," I said as I got up. "Get yourself back in order and get up."

He chuckled thickly. "I think I need a moment."

Grinning, I got up and leaned against his desk, watched him bask in the afterglow. He looked like a big cat stretched out down there, all relaxed and happy. The thought I'd given him that glow made me warm inside. And hungry for more. I played with the ruffles on my boxers and fixed my gaze on him.

"Take your moment, then. Once we get back to your place, I intend to exploit you without mercy."

He chuckled. "Yes, please, ma'am."

Chapter 10

The error of my ways became clear in the car. I thought I'd resolved the Marcus issue back there in the office, but Anthony's increasingly rigid spine said I'd been overly optimistic. Either that or there was some other horror waiting to pounce on me—entirely possible. We sat silently in his car, his hands gripping the steering wheel too firmly for my liking.

"Did something happen with Justine?"

He shook his head. "She's fine. Doug's taking good care of her. I wonder how long it'll take him to admit he's crazy about the woman," he said, suddenly smiling.

"Maybe it's the whole hurt-me-good thing. He's built like a war machine, but he doesn't strike me as the type to dish out pain. It's one of the reasons I trust him."

"You think Justine is that simple? That anyone is?"

I shrugged. "There's a line between playing around like we do and doing pain for real like those guys in the Playroom. Seems pretty simple to me. Don't get me wrong—I'm not saying there's anything wrong with doing whatever floats people's boats—I just don't get it."

He sighed. "You don't have to get it in order to accept it, Beatrice. I don't get you, but I accept you."

Too close to home. "I am that simple, though."

"Are you?"

He looked over at me for one second, sticky questions bubbling up behind his eyes. This was exactly why I liked him all sexed up. The glow was good—the twenty questions were horrible.

"There's nothing simple about anyone, Bea. Sometimes I wish there was. But simple things are rarely fun, are they?"

"If you ask me, there's too much complicated in my life. I like simple. I'd like to do simple, to be able to. Complicated people aren't interesting, they're just difficult. I'd like easy."

He chuckled. "Are you sure? Because you're hanging around me, and I'm not easy. Or am I?"

I stuck my tongue out and pinched his biceps. "Well, I did get you to roll over on the floor a bit earlier. Didn't take a lot of work."

"Nothing easy about that, believe me. I'm not the rolling-over type."

I brushed my hand over his bulging muscles, enjoyed the tingle of his warmth traveling up my wrist. "I know. It makes everything we do together that much better. Because you're not working out one of your kinks, you're doing what you do for me, *with* me. It's intimate and it belongs only to us."

"So if I liked women on top generally, it would make us making love less valuable to you?"

I thought about it. "It would, I think. Because in the back of my mind I'd have this idea that anyone could ride you and it might be all the same. That you enjoy being ridden, not being with me. I know it sounds crazy, but it's how I feel. As it is, I can tell you're dying to get on top of me. That you're dying to ride me. But you hold back, you go that extra mile. For me, *just* for me."

His fingers tapped against the wheel, then he turned to look at me for a moment. "Does that mean that being with me is as good as being with anyone else for you? Just because you want to be on top, that it could be anyone underneath you and it would make no difference?"

Well, damn, framed like that it made no sense. "No. No, it wouldn't be the same."

Because I could let Richie top me, no problem. It was just Anthony that I couldn't stand having over me. Because he touched more than just my body when he touched me. Because his caress meant something more than flesh against flesh. But there was no way to tell him that, was there? No way to make it make sense to him. So I could only hope he'd keep on accepting, if he was so wise about it and all. Accepting me. For a while, at least. For as long as I could keep from running from whatever it was that was happening between us.

"See my point?" he said, all satisfied. "Your being on top is your brand of kink, for whatever reason. The fact you enjoy it with me isn't the same as if you did it with anyone else. I hope."

"Yeah, I guess you're right. I don't inflict pain on you, though."

He sighed. "Is that what you're hung up on? Pain is a very relative notion, you know. Each body perceives it differently, reacts to it differently. Don't think Justine's brand of fun is somehow wrong just because it's not your own."

Maybe he had a point. But it was such a dangerous edge to play with in my mind. Exchanging pain, making it seem all right, even pleasurable. That scared me breathless. Maybe because I was terrified I'd love to dish out some. Maybe because in my mind it would make me a version of my father somehow. I shuddered and fell silent.

"You know, when I first saw you I knew you'd be trouble. That you'd drive me out of my mind, confuse me, excite me. And when I watched you dance, I knew you'd be the hottest thing to touch, the tastiest thing to lick. I wanted you anyway, knowing it would drive me up the wall to have you. Because women like you always drive people up the wall."

"What's that supposed to mean, 'women like me'?"

We stopped at a red light and his eyes fixed on mine. I couldn't look away, though I did try. "Gorgeous women. Scared women. It doesn't take a genius to figure out something scared you bad, sparrow. Still does."

I gulped. "Think Doug and Justine will hook up?"

"Aaah. Deflection again. See, what did I tell you? You drive me up the wall. But I accept you."

For now. I felt it hanging there at the end. But he didn't say it. His eyes stayed glued to the road.

"Maybe they will get together. He doesn't have to give her everything, just enough to keep her satisfied."

I liked that idea so I nodded.

"Can I ask you something, Bea?"

Not good, generally. "Sure."

"Why would you choose your mom's name? Won't it bother her?"

"No, it can't."

He chuckled, but it was nervous more than giddy. "Anything can bother moms. It's one of those universal laws."

"Not mine. Nothing can bother her anymore. She's dead."

Choking silence fell over us in the car. My heart throbbed painfully, chest hurting. I reached out and fumbled with some buttons, desperate for music intervention. Adele sang at me from some radio station and some of the pain subsided. I closed my eyes and allowed her beautiful voice to wash out the despair from my soul.

He stayed silent until the song was over. But I knew it wouldn't last for long.

"I'm sorry," he said gruffly.

"Not as sorry as I am," I said, mirroring his own answer from earlier that day.

"Would you mind if I asked—"

"Yes, I would. I don't want to talk about it. Not yet."

He nodded once and kept staring out as he drove. After a while I settled on looking out the side window. Everything blurred together as we sped through the night. The world around me dissolved to the sound of music. I focused on that until the car stopped moving.

When we got back to his building, he opened the door for me, carried my bag inside. He was tender and caring, and it only made things worse. I turned to go toward the guest bedroom, but his hand caught mine.

"Don't fly away, sparrow," he whispered.

I nibbled on the inside of my cheek. My feet wouldn't step away from him; it was like the damned things had a mind of their own. He dragged us to the living room couch, all the while keeping a firm hold on my hand and caressing me with his thumb.

"I wish I could hug you right now."

I flinched. "Don't."

"I won't, don't panic. But I wish I could. Maybe it would make you feel better. I know for sure it would make *me* feel better."

"I'm sorry," I whispered.

"What for?"

"For being so…"

I trailed away there. A lot of words could have filled the blank space: fucked-up, weird, broken.

"But I need you to understand, Anthony, that I'm not a project. You won't save me from whatever imaginary dragons you think are chasing me. And if those dragons are real, nobody will slay them. Can you accept that?" I exhaled thickly, lips drawing into a tight line.

"I'm doing my best. About that Marcus guy…" he said in a small voice.

That threw me off. "What?"

"I don't think you should encourage him. He's smitten enough to stalk you from what I understand, so if you seem interested, he might think you are. Interested."

"What if he does?"

"Well…it'd be cruel. Because you're with me now. You are, right? With me? Now?"

I squeezed his hand between my palms. "Thought we'd established that back in your office. This is as 'with' anyone as I could ever be."

"But you won't let me love you, will you?"

I was taken aback by the question. It came out of the blue and hit right between my eyes with the force of a baseball bat. "What are you talking about?"

"You won't let me love you. You're keeping me one step away—or more, if you can wiggle the distance in. When we're making love, when we're talking—always. You keep me away. What are you so afraid of?"

"That's not fair, Anthony."

"No, it really isn't."

"I meant it's not fair of you to say that. I'm giving you as much as I can. I'm sorry if it's not enough."

Though I wasn't sure how sorry I really was. I wanted to have him around but I wanted him to go, too. Whiplash. He sighed and leaned back in the couch, eyes brimming with something dangerous. Something scary.

"It's hopeless, isn't it?"

Was I missing something? I felt like I'd walked into the middle of this discussion. "What is?"

"I'm falling hard for you, Beatrice. And you're going to keep pushing me away, because it scares you to be loved. I just wish I knew why that's so terrifying to you."

It wasn't. Him loving me was fine. Me loving him, on the other hand…I shivered.

"I've told you before, don't care about me. And you most certainly shouldn't love me."

"You're cruel, you know?"

My stomach lurched. "No, I'm not. Why would you say that?"

"Forget it. Sleep tight, Bea. I'll see you in the morning."

And just like that he got up and walked into his bedroom. I stood there frowning at his closed door, rehashing everything we'd said. I had no idea where it had all gone so terribly wrong. But then again I didn't know much about relationships. Didn't do well with feelings.

I took my things into the guest bedroom and slouched around for a while. After a shower, I climbed into bed, exhausted and confused. And lonely—something I was used to but that seemed particularly bitter tonight. So I grabbed my phone and hit speed dial.

"Hey, doll. You all right?"

I sighed. "Yeah, long day. How are you? How's Justine?"

"Giving me grief about pills. I swear I'll tie the woman down and feed her these damn things between her gritted teeth."

I chuckled. "Glad you're not my nurse."

"Yeah, well. I'm glad you don't need one. How was Satine tonight?"

"Great. The Cristal guy showed up there."

He snorted. "That was fast. Did that asshole Sam tell him where you were?"

"He wouldn't say. But obviously someone did. Anyway, I told him Sam threatened me. At least he can make himself useful and harass that idiot so he'll leave us all alone. Cristal guy's name is Marcus Forder, by the way." A few beats of silence. "Doug? Are you still there?"

"Marcus Forder is your Cristal guy?"

"Yeah, he gave me his card tonight. Why? You know the man?"

"Who doesn't?"

Me, for one. "Pfffft, tell me about it. I mean, literally, tell me about it. Who is he?"

"Only one of the richest assholes in the tri-state area. One of the shadiest, too."

"Are you sure? He looks like a high-class businessman or something."

"The shady ones always do."

He had a point there. But Marcus was not who I cared about right now.

"Say, Doug…can you give me Anthony's number?"

"Gowl's? Why would you need it? Aren't you staying at his place?"

"Yeah, I am. But I need his number."

"Sure. I'll text it to you when we hang up. You sure everything's okay?"

I smiled. "Yeah, everything's fine."

The phone beeped with Anthony's number a few seconds later. I got it into my phonebook, then called. My stomach fluttered as I heard the ringing from the other room. Was he sleeping? I'd just heard the shower a few minutes ago, so unless he was the world's quickest fall-asleep-er he had to be up. But it took him a while to answer.

"What are you doing, Beatrice?"

He didn't sound upset, just tired. Tired for the day or tired of me already, I couldn't decide.

"I'm sleeping with you."

"Pretty sure I'd know if you were right now. Or was that an invitation?"

"This is the only way I can fall asleep with you."

Rustling sounded over the phone. The bed screeched a bit. I heard that from his room.

"Okay, we're in bed now."

"My door is locked from the inside. I hope you won't take that…personally," I blurted.

He sighed. "There's a lot about us I shouldn't take personally, huh?"

"Yeah, I guess. I'm s—"

"Don't say you're sorry. I'm trying really hard not to blow down your house of straw to reach you."

"Did you just call me a piglet by any chance?"

He chuckled. "That would make me the wolf trying to devour you."

"Let's switch. You be the piglet and I'll be the wolf."

"Ha. Ha. I'm not the one barricading myself, though, am I?"

I turned on my back, stared at the ceiling in the darkness of his guest bedroom. "I'm doing the best I can, Anthony. Please believe that."

"I do, sparrow. I'm doing the best I cannot to cage you in, too. I just hope it'll be enough."

"It has to. It will. Tell me about your sister."

More rustling, then silence. "Will you tell me about your mother if I do that?"

I gulped thickly and bit on the inside of my cheek. He was a tough negotiator. "Fair enough. You go first," I whispered.

"Melissa loved to watch cartoons," he said thickly. "Eighteen and still watched cartoons avidly. They made her laugh. She had a beautiful laugh, throaty and rich. It made me laugh too, no matter how hard I tried to fight it. She used to say she'd become a doc, save lives. Even when she started with the damned drugs, I was sure she'd be all right. That she'd be out of the woods in no time, that it was just a rebelling phase. But somehow she lost her way… and I didn't manage to find her in those dark woods she got lost in. They swallowed her up in the end."

"You feel like you failed her?" I asked in a small voice.

"Yeah. Pretty sure I did—she's not here anymore and she could've been. There's no clearer failing than that, is there?"

"I failed my mom too. It wasn't drugs or anything like that, but I…I didn't know, didn't see. Maybe I didn't want to know and see. And I failed her."

"How long has she been gone?"

Inhale deeply, exhale slowly. "Two years."

"Are you going to make me ask? Or will you tell me?"

It was the easiest thing to drop that bomb, I guessed. So I braced myself and marched into my own dark woods.

"She was…attacked."

"I'm so sorry, Bea. I can't begin to image how that must've affected your family."

Oh, he couldn't begin to imagine—that was right. "It was my father."

"What was?"

"My father attacked her. He…killed her. With a knife. Stabbed her thirty-four times. How much determination, right? I think it's physically exhausting to stab someone thirty-four times. I keep imagining him tired over it; did he coach himself through them? Did he give up in the end out of sheer exhaustion? What makes someone stop after stabbing their spouse thirty-four times?"

"I…don't know what to say. That's…horrifying."

Good pick for someone who didn't know what to say.

"When he was done stabbing her, he killed himself. Right on top of her. He wouldn't even give her a chance to get away in death. And I found them. The way he hugged her in the middle of that pool of blood…I can't get that image out of my head."

I heard his breath over the phone, heavier than before. I took his silence in, allowed it to hug my heart. A shiver went through me at the thought, but there was also comfort there. Fear and comfort—a heady combination and his signature effect on me.

When he spoke again, his voice felt like a caress. "You said you'd tell me when it wouldn't make a difference between us. Does this mean I've lost you?"

I wasn't sure right then. He had more than anyone had ever had, so in many ways he had lost me. I had to make him lose me; anything else scared me speechless. But he could lose me slowly, one day at a time. It didn't have to be all at once. The fear and pleasure at that thought held hands and danced together.

"How would you feel if you did lose me?"

"Pissed off. I didn't even have you properly—I can't lose you already. Right?"

I chuckled. "You're funny when you're pissed off."

He snorted. "Happy to entertain."

I thought about it, but only for a second.

"You didn't lose me. And you do have me, as much as I can be had. Not sure if that's a good thing or not."

"It's a great thing. Because I want you really, really bad."

A curse and a blessing, for both of us. "Anthony?"

"Yeah?"

"I wish you could hug me, too."

"Close your eyes, sparrow. Put the phone by your side on the pillow and close your eyes. I wanna be with you when you fall asleep tonight."

I sucked in air and bit the inside of my cheek hard. Sleeping with someone was a big thing. Not having sex, but sleeping. It was such a big thing that it hollowed my stomach instantly. Even over the phone, from across the hall, it was a big thing. Falling asleep beside someone meant you trusted them enough to fall unconscious beside them. How many times had my mom trusted my father during their years together? How many times had she closed her eyes beside him and allowed him to hold her? My body shook hard and I buried my face in the pillow.

But I didn't hang up.

•••

Morning snuck up on me. I was sleeping deeply when my phone began to ring. I was close to sending it flying into the wall, but when I saw Anthony's name on the display, I decided to give it a second chance. I answered and grumbled into the speaker.

"Good morning to you too," he said, laughing.

"Not funny," I mumbled into the pillow.

"You're definitely not a morning person."

"Us night people recoil from the light of day. Sun burns our eyes and scorches our skin."

He laughed again, but then stopped. "I wanted you to wake up to me."

My eyes shot open and I bit my lip. "And I did. Grumbling like a bear with a sore paw."

"Part of your charm," he quipped.

"Shut up."

"Want breakfast? Come out of your den. I'm waiting for you in the kitchen."

The line went dead. God, I wanted to sleep more. People who got up earlier than they absolutely had to made no sense to me. I threw my legs over the edge of the bed and ran a hand over my face. That was a lucky break, finding my face. After a shower I felt more or less human, but I wasn't entirely there yet.

My armor of choice was a pair of sweats and a top.

"Sexy," he said, chuckling from the other side of the table.

"You want sexy? Give me three more hours of sleep and I'll consider it."

A big mug of coffee winked at me, and I was quick to snatch it up.

"Hey, that was mine!"

"Tough luck," I muttered between sips.

The nectar of the gods glided down my throat and slowly pushed my lids up all the way. It was too morning, very bright. I hated bright. It meant I was up way too early. I squinted at him. "So what's next, a stake through the heart? Garlic attack?"

He rolled his eyes and pushed a plate of steamy scrambled eggs in my direction. "Not unless you like garlic with your eggs."

"Nah, it's fine."

"Can I have my coffee back now?"

I considered it, inspected his face. Then grinned. "No. Get your own."

"*That* was my own."

I *tsked*. "You have clear issues with sharing. We'll work on that."

His dark eyes flashed scary-intense, and I gulped. "I don't share, sparrow."

The moment turned entirely too intense for morning—well, any time of the day really—so I scrunched my nose at him. "This coffee mug is not leaving my ever-loving hands, man."

He smiled softly and the moment was gone. I had mixed feelings about it, but then I had more coffee and all was right with the world. He got up, walked away, and came back with a beautiful white rose. Instead of making a big deal out of it, he just left it by my side on the table and sat back down in his chair with a paper open wide. I dug into the eggs, sighed as they hit my tongue.

"You're an awesome cook." I talked around my fork.

"Scrambled eggs aren't exactly the height of cuisine."

I decided I loved his hands. They looked strong as he held the newspaper, a firm grip. But they were also hands that had made me breakfast and brought me a beautiful white rose. It made me smile. Running a hand over the petals brought tingles from my fingertips to my stomach.

"Thanks," I whispered.

"Whatever I can do for you, it's my pleasure."

Mornings generally seemed overrated to me, just like small talk. I got myself a refill of coffee and settled in the chair. He kept reading and the craziest impulse came over me. I started poking at the paper, at first softly but then harder and harder as he kept focusing on it. No use, though I could see the corners of his lips trying to twitch up with each new poke. But he seemed determined to read that damn paper. So I got up, walked to his chair, and straddled him, hooking my arms around his neck.

He chuckled when I poked my nose at his.

"Morning," I whispered against his lips.

"Morning, beautiful. Is it okay if I touch you?"

I nodded against his cheek. "Just don't close your arms over me."

His palms felt hot as they ran up my legs from knees to thighs and rested there, strong fingers rubbing softly against my hips. I bit my lip and decided it was much better to nip at *his* lower lip.

"Thanks for the rose. It's beautiful."

He tipped his head back, gave me more space to play with his lips. I dragged one of them between mine, sucking on it. He moaned and flexed his fingers on my hips. I loved feeling him hard and hot under me.

"You mentioned exploiting me without mercy last night."

The deep voice ran down my spine and made me tingly all over. "Volunteering?"

"Yes, please."

I brushed my lips against his a few times before kissing him in earnest. He tasted of coffee and I loved that, so I dipped in deeper and fed on the mix of his taste and that of delicious, dark coffee.

My breakfast of champions.

Chapter 11

Things got worse as the day went on, though. After I rode him hard in the morning, his eyes turned sad, sadder as we ran into little things. Like taking a shower together, or a bath—I didn't like the idea of that small space and the dynamics of the two of us fitting into a tub. It wasn't just a no, but a hell no. Each time I tried to make it up to him, it got worse. He'd get another freak-out-generating idea—it seemed like he only had that kind.

By the time we got to the club that evening, he was twitching in his own skin, brusque and mostly silent. I walked into his office with my bag and the freshly cleaned costume. He turned to walk away but I grabbed his arm.

"Please stay."

He sighed heavily, dark eyes giving me the chills. It hacked at my heart to see him sad. I leaned in closer, gulped repeatedly as he hovered over me, and tipped my head back. My heart threatened to burst free of my chest, pulse jumping painfully through my body. His gaze danced over my face and he ran a fingertip over my lips, smiled that humorless smile of his that tormented me.

"I'm making it worse, huh?" I whispered dejectedly. "What can I do to make you smile for real?"

The sadness hurt because I felt like I'd put it there. I couldn't stand the thought.

"It's not your fault. I'm just pissed off I keep pushing you, even though I'm trying not to. It kills me when you flinch, or chew on the inside of your cheek, or bite your nails."

"Biting nails is perfectly acceptable!" I said, mock-frowning. "And I don't chew on my cheek, just…casually nibble."

He kept caressing my lips with his fingertips. "I guess it's just going to take time. I'll get used to your limits, you'll get used to having me around. Right?"

"I'm not going anywhere. Unless you start showing—"

"Saggy Butt Syndrome, got it," he said, finally grinning.

I frowned. "You really love cutting my lines short. I find it highly irritating."

"Do you? Where, precisely, are you irritated? Show me the spot."

I stuck my tongue out and began pulling my clothes off. He licked his lips, took a few steps back.

"No, don't go. Stand leaning against your desk."

He frowned. "That would mean looming, though."

It didn't feel like I'd freak out over it. Of course, if I was wrong I'd soon find out. I faced him as I dropped my clothes, one item at a time. My pulse spiked insanely, and I could see his excitement tenting his pants. I licked my lips so much they began to chafe. After pulling on the panties, settling the corset and fishnet stockings, I grabbed the ruffly red boxers. Inhaled deeply, exhaled slowly. My head got all clear as air rushed at my brain.

"Now keep very, very still…" I whispered and turned around.

Bending down, I made sure to give him a tasty view as I got the ruffles on. He swallowed thickly when my costume was all in place. I picked up the gloves, turned around to face him, and pulled them on, staring at him. The crimson high heels rested beside me and I grinned. Picking them up, I walked to one of the chairs, sat down slowly. I did keep chewing at my lips and the inside of my cheek, but I didn't freak out. He was standing over me, tall, wide, hungry. So hungry it radiated off him. I felt his desire wash over me, wave after wave. I fed on it, relished its taste in the back of my mouth.

"You sure this is okay?" he asked gruffly.

"Hmmm…almost. I need the shoes. Pick them up and put them on for me."

He made to kneel but I stuck a foot on his groin, making him freeze in place. "Don't kneel. I'll reach my feet up."

He nodded and clutched at my shoes. "There's something endlessly erotic about a woman with her feet up."

I rolled my eyes but shivered as the first shoe slid in place, then the second. There was something endlessly erotic about him, especially right now. My heart fluttered funny and my throat was dry. "You're hard."

He chuckled tightly. "A recurring condition when I'm around you."

Hmm…"I want to watch you get off."

His eyes became even darker, if that were possible. He cleared his throat, blushed a little. I was going to ruin my panties for sure.

"You mean…now? Here?"

"Now. Here." I purred.

He took himself out, touched his flesh while staring at me. I leaned back in the chair and fixed my gaze on him. I wanted to taste him again, to feel him throb inside me. I wanted to have him and him to have me. My eardrums buzzed as his movement sped up.

"Wait," I muttered thickly.

Leaning over, I pulled his hand before me and started to lick it, making it all slick and slippery for him. The thought of him touching his flesh while something of me was there made me feel all hot and bothered. His hand returned to rub at his hot length when I was done. I focused on his harsh breath, on the angry flare of the tip of him. When he was about to come I reached out one of my wet wipes. I loved watching him clean himself up and arrange his pants and shirt.

"Good as new."

His voice was deep but soft, like a caress. He sounded happy, looked happy. I liked that look on him a lot better than the one he'd been carrying around all day. This was what I wanted to give him—smiles, pleasure, that glow. This was what I wanted him to have.

"I'll dance thinking of that. All night, I'll move and sway thinking of you touching yourself."

"Hmmm…maybe I can look forward to some merciless exploiting when we get home tonight."

"Maybe."

His beautiful dark eyes turned from playful to serious in the blink of an eye. "Give me a chance, Bea. Just one chance, I'm not asking for more."

I was so tired all of a sudden. My shoulders slumped and I leaned back in the chair. "I'm a coward," I mumbled.

"No, you're not. You're very brave because you're taking a chance on me."

I snorted. "Love your optimism. Maybe I need some time and—"

"You need to let me love you, that's what you need. You need to let me in."

"What if I can't?"

He walked closer, slowly bent over resting his palms on the armrests on either side of me. His lips touched my forehead, brushed against my nose. He tipped my head back, and I shivered all over as he kissed me slowly. My skin tingled with his nearness.

"Sure you can. You'll try hard for me, for us. Won't you?"

"Maybe I won't be able to try hard enough."

"I'm just asking you to try, sparrow."

I sighed and pushed my forehead into him. "We'll negotiate after we get home tonight, okay?"

He chuckled. "I love how that sounds."

"Of course you do. You're a very pushy, demanding man, aren't you? Stubborn to the core."

"Oh, yeah. But I'm glad I am, because it takes a lot of will to reach you."

"It's not worth the effort. There's no pot of gold at the end of this rainbow."

He *tsked*. "You're worth it."

The discussion was way too heavy. "You're just trying to get into my pants."

He laughed and tipped my chin up with a finger. "Always."

"Glad you've got your priorities straight."

"Damn right," he quipped. "Now go out there and take everyone's breath away."

I pushed up from the chair, curved my spine out. Yeah, I'd do just that.

Marcus was up there at his table. The Cristal would most likely be at the end of the stairs down from my cube by the end of the night. I'd glow with the joy of a night spent dancing. I could count on these small things to make the night right, to build up my courage to go on. To try. It was way too early to give up; it was something I decided on each night right after I took my first bow to the crowd.

After dancing for a while, I noticed a familiar face in the crowd: Tony with his trademark cig hanging from his lips. He nodded at me, and when I was done with my number for the night I walked up to him.

"Need to talk," he shouted over the still-blaring music.

Anthony wasn't around. I didn't want to go back into his office if he wasn't there. The Marcus situation had been lesson enough— doors that could be closed and men didn't mix well.

"Let's go out back."

He walked after me to the alley beside Leather & Chains. It wasn't that dark—some streetlight made its way there. That was how I noticed something glinted in his hand.

"Tony? What's that?"

"You need to come back. Sam said he's going to kill you."

My heart began to pound. A terrible feeling took root in the pit of my stomach. "Why are you holding a knife?"

The cig hung limply between his lips as he smiled. "To keep you safe. In case Sam shows up."

His eyes didn't look right. Bloodshot, frantic…he kept looking around, knife fidgeting in his hand. This was Tony, but it wasn't the Tony I knew. That scared the hell out of me.

"I'm going back in."

"NO!" he shouted.

I winced and took a step back. His eyes narrowed into slits.

"Don't take another step. You're coming back to the Pearl. This is all wrong. Why didn't you call me for help? Why didn't you turn to me when shit hit the fan? Think these people care about you? Nobody cares like I do. You're coming back to me."

I shook my head. "It was you, wasn't it? Not Sam. It was all you."

"That asshole had no idea what sort of jewel he had under his roof. I tried to make you shine the brightest. You were my jewel."

"Tony, you look tired. You look exhausted. How about we go back down, sit and talk about it? You don't want to do this."

All those nights we'd sat at the bar together, drinking something and just being there. No small talk, no effort to fill silence with chatter. I'd thought him almost a friend. I'd almost trusted him. And he was holding a knife to me, appeared quite decisive about using it. My mind flashed to the horrible image of my parents, of my father's knife. Irony was a bitch and she sure loved me. Why couldn't things be easy? Just for freaking once. I gulped and looked around. I thought something moved beside the door just as a couple of cars passed by the alley's entrance, music blaring.

"It's this asshole here, isn't it? He's got you all fooled. I bet he's into that kinky shit, whipping and tying you up. Does he tie you up when he fucks you?"

He licked his lips, eyes fixed on my ruffles. Bile bubbled in my stomach. I focused on breathing, tried to think. How was I going to get out of this? He was big. I wasn't exactly skilled at one-on-one combat let alone dealing with knives. As far as I was concerned, I'd need some ninja skills to get out of this clusterfuck.

"I could do that to you, tie you up. Beat you. You'd like that, wouldn't you? You'd get off on it just like that leathered up bitch. She put these ideas in your head."

"You beat Justine up. How could you?"

He sneered. "The bitch got what she deserved. I think she loved getting it. I might find her on my doorstep with all her shit. Though she didn't see my face, so she can't, huh? I don't want her, anyway. I want you."

"Tony…"

"Stop calling my name. Now you tell me, you tell me straight. Are you like that bitch now? Will you get off on me hurting you? I wanna hurt you right now. I'd hurt you real good, make your pussy all wet."

I heaved, clutched at my mouth. There was a stack of pizza boxes beside me. If I managed to throw them at him maybe he'd get scared. Maybe I could slip away, run into the street. The main street was behind him, but the club's main entrance was the other way. My hand shot out and threw those boxes at him. I turned around and ran for the main entrance as fast as my high-heeled feet would carry me.

He cursed and shouted for me to stop, ran after me. His heavier steps thudded on the pavement behind me. They sounded so much louder than they could have been, much too close. I couldn't breathe. *Please, God, not a knife. Let it be anything else but a knife.*

The guy at the main entrance saw me first, then Tony with the knife. He got up and put his body in front of mine. I just shrunk there behind him, heart thudding painfully in my eardrums.

"You wanna turn around and go," the bouncer said calmly.

I knew Anthony had called him something, but I couldn't remember what. Did he mean me or Tony? My knees wouldn't allow me to take one more step. Tony didn't look like he wanted to chat. But then again he never really did.

"I wanna peel the skin off of your face, little shit. That's what I wanna do. This is between her and me, stay the fuck out."

The bouncer shook his head. I watched the spiky blond hair move around as he did, found his entire presence way too interesting. I was willing to focus on anything except Tony, pretty much. "Varana is every bit my business."

"Who the fuck is Varana?" Tony bellowed.

I closed my eyes and wished really hard I wasn't there. Or that I had some hardcore ninja skills and I could kick his ass. Wearing ruffles, a corset, and high heels didn't really go with that whole ninja vibe.

A sizzling sound and some groans got my attention. I peeked out from behind the bouncer to see Tony twitching on the ground and Marcus grinning down at him. He held something in his hand that looked very much like a stun gun.

"Good thing I didn't leave right away," Marcus said, looking up.

Well. A good thing would've been me kicking Tony's ass. Marcus doing it was an okay thing, I guessed. It sure beat Tony stabbing me or anyone else. The bouncer stepped away from me to reach the slumped body on the ground. He picked Tony up and began to walk away, dragging the still body with him.

"Hey, shouldn't we call the police?" I called after him.

"Nah. I'll take him personally, make sure he gets there all right," he said over his shoulder.

I seriously and sincerely doubted that, but I wasn't overcome with care for Tony right then. Marcus walked up to me.

"You okay? Did he…?"

"No. I ran away, and then you did the…thing. I'm fine."

Anthony jogged out of the building. "What happened? James said someone tried to attack you?"

He looked sort of frantic, eyes wide. I stepped closer to him, pushed my hands up his chest until they reached his neck. It took some pulling, but he finally bent down a little so I could kiss him. It wasn't to calm him down. It was to calm me down. My hands and knees were shaking, blood still rushing through my veins. My body felt all jumpy, and yet I wanted to slump there in his arms.

Marcus cleared his throat. "I'm happy I caught the bastard in time. He looked raving mad."

"He is raving mad," I whispered.

I stepped away from Anthony but leaned on his shoulder.

"I've been talking to Sam," Marcus said after a heavy sigh. "I think Tony has been lying to you for a while. Sam was under the impression you and Tony were a couple. What I mean is Tony gave him that impression. Said you kept changing costumes because Tony liked to see you in new ones."

"The bastard! I kept changing them because he told me Sam asked!"

Anthony's arm crept around me slowly. The warmth didn't freak me out—it brought me comfort. I sighed heavily and settled closer against him. My feet weren't really willing to support my weight anymore.

"He pulled a knife on me," I mumbled. "We've known each other for a year, hung out a lot, drank together. I thought he was okay, you know, a normal person. And he pulled a knife on me. Is everyone out of their goddamn minds?"

Anthony's body turned into stone. "You're sure you're okay?"

"Yeah, I threw some pizza boxes at him and ran. But he looked insane. He would've…"

"Don't think about that," Marcus jumped in. "I'll make sure he won't bother you again."

Anthony's chest puffed out. "Kind of you to offer, but we can handle it."

"Yes, you probably can. But nobody would ask me any questions."

"Guys, are you done with the pissing contest? Let's nip it in the bud here. Anthony, I wanna go home."

"Sure, let's go. Thanks for being here, Marcus. You're my best friend from here on."

He chuckled and shook Anthony's hand. "I think I'd like to be Varana's best friend."

Varana didn't need best friends. The real one had no use for them anymore since she was dead. The fake one, me, didn't know what to do with one. And he wasn't interested in friendship, obviously. But I smiled up at him either way. He had just taken a psycho down with style.

Anthony carried me to his car. Technically, I sort of walked. But really, I leaned on him so much he might as well have been carrying me around.

"Are you sure he didn't hurt you? With the adrenaline buzz you might've not noticed."

"You're welcome to check," I mumbled against his chest.

"Was that a joke or real permission?"

I shrugged. "Whatever works for you."

He sat me down in the passenger's seat of his car, legs dangling out of the side. Kneeling before me, he inspected with slow attention every inch of skin and fabric he could reach. I was pretty sure I wasn't hurt, but him fussing over me felt right. It brought me comfort.

"I'm so sorry I wasn't there."

I pushed a hand under his chin and tilted his face up. "We're not joined at the hip. Don't blame yourself."

He gulped. "That maniac could have…"

"He didn't. Let's focus on that."

"You're taking this very well," he said carefully.

"Heh. Give me half an hour or so, it'll hit then. I process things a bit slower than they happen. Take me home, okay?"

He flinched. "You mean to your apartment?"

The idea hadn't occurred to me, to be honest. But right then, as he said it, I knew that was what I wanted. I needed the comfort of my small apartment. I needed to know Doug lived next door, even if he wasn't home. Hopefully he wasn't the kind of friend to pull a knife on me at some point. I shuddered.

"Yeah, let's go to my apartment. Hurry."

He helped me fix my legs in the car, closed the door, and rushed around to get behind the wheel. My body began to shake harder and harder as he drove. By the time we reached my apartment door, I stared stupidly at the lock.

"I don't…don't have the keys. My bag…"

"I have it. Want me to unlock the door?"

I nodded and leaned against the wall. It made me think of Richie, oddly enough. He usually did the leaning against walls. In light of new events, I had a special kind of respect for men who didn't care enough to turn obsessive. Too bad he turned violent because of booze. But it was impersonal violence, so it rated as less evil on my scale of things.

Anthony opened the door and gave me space to walk in. I almost stumbled but appreciated the fact he didn't try to touch me unless I reached for him. I needed a bit of distance.

"I need to lie down," I mumbled, shivering.

"Okay. I'll be here in the living room. You just say my name, and I'll be right there with you."

His dark eyes looked haunted. It seemed cruel somehow to push him away. I knew it would bring him comfort to comfort me, to take care of me. But I couldn't stand it right now. Tony's vicious eyes kept making rounds through my head.

"Anthony, I need you to stay out here. In the living room. But don't leave. Please."

He nodded and watched me as I stumbled into the bedroom. I didn't bother taking the shoes off, instead plopping down on my bed with the costume on and everything. Even the hat. It was pinned safely to my hair anyway.

My body just melted into the mattress. It smelled of me, of my lonely days. I wanted Anthony's smell to claim the sheets and pillows, but right now the thought of being touched made me shake harder. The more my body rebelled against the idea, the worse the need for him got. Fear and craving, so different yet all the same. My heart thumped each time I remembered Anthony touching me. His taste invaded my mouth, and my muscles began to slowly relax. It was a good thing to focus on.

I was back on my feet before I knew it, zombie-ing out of the bedroom and into the small living room.

Chapter 12

Once I got there, the walls were closing in on me. I wanted to leave, not sure where I'd go. The crazed look on Tony's face flashed through my mind again.

"Beatrice?"

I almost didn't hear him, my thoughts were so loud. How could I have been so wrong about Tony? Why didn't I see he wasn't right? I kept worrying my hands, muscles twitchy and tense. All the while I'd been trying to keep Anthony away, fearing the worst about him. What if he hid a monster deep inside too? We all did, I thought bitterly. All of us hid hideous monsters deep inside. Some, like Tony, lost control over it, and it possessed them.

Anthony stood there by the couch, his eyes brimming with something that made my lungs freeze.

"Please, don't look at me like that," I whispered.

I swallowed nervously and looked around. I could get out that door if I'd just get him to move maybe four feet away …

"Beatrice. Sparrow."

"Don't call me that!" I snapped. "Not now. Step aside, just give me space."

"I can't let you run away. Not now, not when you're like this."

"I'm not your little pet project, Anthony Gowl. Step away from the goddamn door."

Something about him changed. His eyes shone a glassy black and arrested my breath. "No."

He spoke it simply, calmly. Almost resigned to whatever he was going to inflict on me. I felt in the pit of my stomach that this was going to be bad.

"What are you doing?" I said in a trembling voice.

He turned around, locked all the locks on my front door—they were many—and turned toward me with finality. The keys disappeared into his pocket. Some of the locks could be opened from the inside, no keys. Some needed a key regardless of which side of the door you stood on. I was locked in. Trapped. This was it. He wasn't going to let me flutter away; he'd give me no more space. The cage was closing around me. I choked on air.

"Please, don't do this now. I need to…leave. Give me that key and step away from the door. I'm asking you nicely," I said, shivering.

His face was set in stone. It was that finality that scared me the worst. "No," he said softly.

I froze there, eyes wide and body shivering like a leaf. His gaze fixed on mine and froze my blood up. He walked closer slowly, one step at a time.

"I'm in love with you, Beatrice Stevens. I can't let you run away every time things get complicated. Tonight you'll either let me in or run away from me forever. I need a solution, a scratch to this itch that's devouring my heart."

I shuddered. "Tonight? I can't…"

His eyes showed no mercy. I blinked a couple of times, bit my lip hard enough to taste copper. Nothing stopped him—one step at a time he closed in on me. I stepped back until I bumped into the wall. I expected a freak-out to explode, but sadly it didn't. All I could feel was a sick need and a craving vibrating through my bones. My blood pulsed impatiently despite the trembling in my knees.

When he finally reached me, he opened his arms slowly. As if to warn me, to make it clear that he'd go there. That he'd ignore all my barriers and walls. Just him opening his arms shattered layers of my comfort.

I shook my head, eyes wide. "Don't do this. I don't want you to do this right now…"

"I can't control my heart, Bea. I love you. I need you. Do you understand? I need you. And it's either have you or lose you, no middle ground. No haven from this tormenting need. You'll either love or hate me, Bea. I can't stand anything else. Tonight is as good as any to decide. Better, in fact. If you don't let me in tonight, you never will."

My body shook violently when his heat enveloped me. Bones melted away as his arms settled on either side of my shoulders. He pushed slowly in, eating the space that kept me sane. My heart beat violently in my ribcage, threatening to break bones and fly away.

When his arms slowly crawled up my hands, I gritted my teeth and froze. He reached my shoulders, pushed between me and the wall to sneak his warm hands around my back. I saw it all happen in slow motion, my body falling into his, shivering and pitiful as it was. Tears welled down my face as he closed his strong arms around me, pulling me into his chest and wrapping around my body like I was a part of him he'd been missing all this time. I whimpered as he squeezed me tight; my body shook violently and I cried out with an inhuman sound, broken and chilling.

"Don't let go," I whispered hoarsely.

"I won't let go," he kept saying over and over again.

I couldn't think straight. Fear and yearning circled each other through my veins, through my mind. There'd be no winner, maybe no loser either. Though my lungs worked overtime with my insane breathing, no freak-out came. I whined like a broken piece of metal, screechy and rusty. He just held me there, squeezed me tighter and tighter into his body until I didn't know if we were separated by skin anymore.

His warmth washed through me, transformed my body into a tight string vibrating with his every breath. I knew what he was about to do before he knew it himself. I willed him to do it. My clothes disappeared as if by magic, my skin goose bumped and threatening to jump off me.

"I'm going to make love to you," he said.

It wasn't hungry, not even then. I felt his need pulse through me, commanding and impatient, but it wasn't greed that drove him. The warmth of his every touch poked at my soul, crawled through the empty spaces in my heart and filled me with an odd kind of joy. This was who we were, our most naked selves. Me scared, him needing to comfort. We'd either come out of it as new people together or break irreparably in the process. I was willing to break right then, high on the madness of him—of us.

His mouth burned as it closed over mine, his tongue unrelenting as it explored and invaded every inch of me. His taste caressed my tongue and spread slowly through my entire body, teasing my hunger for him and making the flames dance higher. His height was overwhelming, and right then I perversely loved the way it made me shiver. His torso was thick and muscular, gorgeous to look at. It made my spine tingle, my insides throb and jump. Strong arms clutched at me desperately, and he caressed and teased every exposed bit of skin, careful to always hold on to me. I was caged, as good as tied down. It felt goddamn glorious.

His fingers dug between my legs, rubbed at my core insistently yet tenderly. I mewled into his throat as my wetness spread over his fingers, the friction and slickness driving me close to mad.

"I'll make love to your soul, to your body, to everything I can touch and get into. And you'll feel me in each and every part of your being."

I gasped as his fingers glided inside me, thick and demanding. *Please…Please, stop, please don't stop.* I moaned open-mouthed and he seemed to crave the taste of it. His mouth latched onto mine and swallowed each and every whimper and moan as his fingers played with my wet folds and made the fire inside worse, almost unbearable. He wrapped one arm under my butt and lifted me up on him, and then we were moving. I didn't care where or how, I just knew I wanted him to take everything. To take it all from me, to pillage and mark something wild that was unraveling inside my very core. I found myself splayed on the coffee table in his living room, my thighs pressed wide apart. His dark eyes fixed on my folds, his tongue sliding out to touch his lips slowly.

"So wet for me…," he said gruffly.

"Don't stop."

I arched my back and my arms shot out to grab his head, pulling him to me. He latched onto my core and sucked greedily, making me scream. I writhed under his assault, whimpered as fingers began to push inside me, teasing me. More, more, I needed more. I tried to say as much but it came out as a jumbled screech. He grinned, danger dripping off of his lips as he pulled back from me. I watched him through half-lidded eyes as he set his tip at my entrance. His dark eyes fixed on mine and he thrust in deeply, savagely. I screamed and arched off the table, taking him deeper inside. I felt myself pulse around him, a terrible itch eating at the bottom of my heart. His upper body folded itself over me slowly, almost in slow motion. I shivered and thrust my arms out, grabbing at him, pulling him closer, sticking my nails into his flesh. He groaned deeply and stuck his arms under my armpits, his hands gripping my head from underneath.

"Please," I rasped out. "Take me hard, please…please…"

His hips drove into me, each thrust reverberating through my soul. I keened, whined, moaned, a sweaty, hot mess underneath him. I licked at his throat, at his lips, at his ear, at whatever I could reach. Nothing was enough. More, I had to have more. I had to have him deeper. The pace of his hips turned almost punishing, the delicious torture singing through my veins. It felt like a statement, like signing the deed to his property, like claiming his grounds. The harder he pushed inside me, the more I came apart under him. His arms tightened around me, sweat making our bodies slide hotly one against the other. We were breathing hard, so very hard. Despair and delight hung there right on the edge of my lips, fear he'd pull out and need to have him deeper inside, even deeper inside. I wanted, needed to feel only him, to know only him, only this insane, burning version of us.

His hips began to lose rhythm and he pushed into me with despair, his hot breath falling over my throat. His lips opened and his teeth scraped against my neck. They closed greedily over my flesh, and his arms tightened around me like a vise. I exploded in a way I never had before, the tidal wave washing through every single part of my body, building and boiling as it went, scraping me raw all over inside. When the explosion finally reached between my legs I arched off the table, shuddered and jumped like a fish out of water, thrashed under him as he held me down and kept pumping inside. I screamed, deeply, hoarsely, insanely. I clawed at him, bit into his shoulder until my teeth hurt from the pressure. He came inside me, a burst of warmth and peace that slowly washed through each part of my soul and fed my body something it had been starving for. I shuddered under him as he held on for dear life, his face buried deep into the crook of my neck.

The shock and shudders of what had happened kept jumping between us for a long while. My muscles dissolved into mush under him, and the weight of his body gave me endless comfort.

"I love you," I whispered.

"Oh, God, I love you too."

His arms tightened around me and I clutched at his head. Everywhere our bodies touched electrical currents still ran through me. He pulled away and I shook, tightening my grip.

"Don't…," I hissed.

"Shh, we're moving into the bedroom."

I swallowed thickly as he got to his feet. He was so beautiful, so strong and intense and mine…it messed with my head. He pulled me up and took me in his arms, clutched at me deliciously.

"I'm going to make love to you all night, sparrow. And hold you, and caress you, and feel you're mine."

I shivered and pressed my head against his shoulder as he carried me. Once we reached my bed, the smell of him assaulted my head from every direction. I could almost see it wrapping around my sheets, my pillows. My chest heaved with it, my body thrived on it. I dug my head into the pillow and coiled around him as soon as he was within reach. His arms wrapped tightly around me, pulled me beside him.

"Are you ready," he whispered.

I knew what he meant. I could read it in his body language. He got up on his knees, maneuvered me right under him and slowly pressed his body down on mine. His chest pushed against my stiff nipples, his hard member poked at my folds. I shivered all over, undulated under him. My heart stuttered as he kissed and licked at my throat, rubbing up slowly against my wetness. I was a mess of him and me inside, but I relished the fact instead of dreading it. I burned thinking there was still something of him lodged inside me, my body, my soul.

He buried himself inside again and again, demanding, hungry, determined. He made love to me hard and fast, slow and deliberate, drove me insane and made me lose my mind over and over and over again. Him on top of me, me on top of him, spooning, reaching, yearning. By the end of it all, I was a sloppy mess of bliss, and he radiated a sort of happiness I had never witnessed, known, or imagined. His lips were hot and dry as he kissed me, slowly, thoroughly. I opened myself to him, welcomed and received him inside, fed on the taste of his mouth.

He coiled his body around mine like a cocoon, hugged me as close as skin would allow without merging into one being. Our hearts slowly calmed down, our breaths coming down from desperate panting back to semi-normal breathing.

"I'm not letting go of you," he stated.

I chuckled and pushed into his chest, wanting him to wrap himself around me tighter, like a shawl.

"Don't want you to. I couldn't stand it if you did. It's like I'm almost fixed when we're together."

"I don't want to fix you, Bea. Human beings can't be fixed. They're not cars or clocks that anyone can mend. You don't need to be 'fixed.' I want you to know I love you as you are now, not some abstract idea of you or of us. I love your taste, your touch, the smell of your skin, and the way you cling to me when I'm inside the heat of your body."

I bit my lip. "But I'm not…whole. I'm just the leftovers of a soul."

"Perfect, because you're the parts I've been missing. I need you beside me so I can be a full soul, baby. Don't walk away. I'm not a full creature without you. Please, don't walk away. Don't run away."

I sighed and dug my nose into his cheek. "Right now I wouldn't be able to crawl away even if I wanted to."

My skin sang with delight everywhere we touched. I'd been yearning for him this way, not knowing what I needed. Not daring to ask for it, to allow the thought to fully form. Tucked into his body, I almost forgot about Tony's betrayal. I almost ignored how scared it made me that I'd been so miserably wrong about someone, again.

"I'll get you the pill tomorrow morning," he mumbled. "I got so carried away that I…"

I shook my head. "Don't. If I get pregnant because you made love to me tonight, then I'll make you a stubborn little baby."

My gut clenched as he fell silent. His palm passed slowly over my cheeks, my lips, even my nose and forehead. "You'd have my baby?" he asked in a small, timid voice.

"Would you want me to?"

He shook and tightened his hold on me. "It would make me deliriously happy, sparrow."

I chuckled and cuddled into him. I didn't think it would happen any time soon, but hearing him say it made me feel lighter inside. If I'd turn out to be wrong about him like I'd been about Tony, or my father, then I'd crash and burn. If I were to crash and burn at some point, I'd feel better knowing it was because of him. At least I'd have tried, I'd have broken the circle of fear. I was brave right then, brazen. It was easy to feel that way when all I could feel inside and outside was him, his strength, his warmth. Tomorrow morning might be different, but for right now, for tonight, I was brave.

"Anthony?"

"Hm?"

"I want you to take me somewhere tomorrow."

"Sure thing. Where are we going?"

"To see my parents."

He fell silent for a while, kept caressing me tenderly. "Are you sure?" he whispered.

"Yeah. I…I haven't seen them in two years. I didn't even go to the funeral. They were buried together, you know? Had that request in their wills, so they buried them together. I couldn't stand the thought of him being there with her."

"We'll go see them tomorrow then. Thanks for wanting to go with me."

I inhaled deeply and allowed air to slide back out. "To be honest, I'm going to use you as support. Not sure I could see them otherwise. But I feel like I need to break free from some sort of invisible chains. And seeing them might open that lock."

"Bea, I'm sorry about Tony."

I flinched. "I'm sorry I didn't realize how sick he was. I just thought he was so chilled out, so cool. Never would've pegged him for a wacko."

"He'll go away for a while, maybe get some help. Though I'm not sure I want the bastard to get help, not sure if he deserves it."

"Everybody deserves help," I whispered.

He hugged me closer, ran a hand through my hair. "You're a very caring, generous soul. You know that?"

"Don't think so."

"Yes, you are. I think there's a lot more heart in you than you give yourself credit for."

I chuckled nervously. "You're just saying that to get into my pants."

He snorted and kissed the bridge of my nose. "Thanks for the confidence. Now let's get some shuteye, hm?"

I took in the warmth of his voice, fed on it. I'd need that tomorrow. It wasn't worth it to live in fear, constantly running away or hiding. Didn't protect me from anything, obviously. In fact maybe it made it worse. Maybe if I'd had friends someone would've noticed Tony wasn't quite right.

I fell into a sleep deep enough to closely resemble a coma. It was the best rest I'd had in years, cradling my soul as well as my body and filling all the small pockets of my being.

Chapter 13

I got up first in the morning. Obviously I was traumatized; getting up earlier than absolutely necessary was way beyond my norm. I tucked a hand under my head and stared at his chest rising and falling. He snored a little in a way that made me chuckle. Romantic movies never showed that. Nobody snored in those perfect little happily-ever-after worlds. Nobody farted or burped, nobody smelled bad. Like I did right now. It had been a long and intense night, and I felt sticky all over. But I couldn't bring myself to get up from beside him, not yet.

It wasn't a perfect picture. It didn't have to be. His lips were softly parted—they looked warm and dry and I longed to lick at them. My chuckling died down as I saw the sheet tenting around his hips. Forget chuckling—my throat dried. I got up slowly, tried my best to keep the bed from whining as I moved. I pulled the sheets down from him, loving the way he squirmed a bit in the open air of the room. The sun shone through a few cracks in my blinds, and those stray beams of light fell around his torso and groin. As if I needed more incentive. I slowly set one knee to the side of him, swinging the second to the other side. He felt hot against my naked body, inviting. I rubbed down slowly, lazily.

"And I thought you weren't a morning person," he said thickly, still keeping his eyes closed.

I chuckled and kept petting myself against him. I wanted to have him, no rush or urgency. Just pleasure, the joy of feeling him in and around me. I wanted to feel only him all over, wanted my world to be filled with his scent, taste, warmth. His hands crawled over my thighs and pulled me harder against him. I bit my lip when he settled his head right on the pillow. His beautiful dark hair stuck out funny in places, all ruffled from sleep. But laughing now wouldn't be too sexy. Besides, all the humor left me as I looked into his eyes. He had a way of sucking the air out of my lungs with one gaze.

He parted his lips and pushed up against me, the friction turning unbearably hot. "What do you have to say for yourself in light of this major lapse in routine?"

I fluttered my eyelashes. "Good morning?"

He smiled. "The best."

I slid down his length then laid down on his chest. His arms came around me, slowly closed over my back and held me there tightly. I shuddered all over, and the pace of his hips increased. I came hard and fast, and he was right there with it, joining me. We stayed like that a while, me still on top of him and his arms holding me close, even closer than before.

"Thank you," he whispered against the top of my hair.

"What for?"

"For trusting me. I'm sure it couldn't have been easy."

"Nothing ever is," I mumbled, pushing my lips against his chest. "It's going to be a day-by-day battle to trust you, Anthony. Right now I'm just giving you the benefit of the doubt."

"The best you can do is all I could wish for, sparrow. We'll take it one day at a time."

My chest constricted painfully and I shivered. One of his arms kept me prisoner against him while the other began to caress down my back. "I love touching you. Holding you like this."

Muscles jumped as his hand touched magic points on my skin. I was starved for physical contact; my skin trembled with joy as he caressed me all over. And yet I was still scared—somewhere in the back of my mind the fear refused to dissolve. How well did I know him? Almost not at all. This was reckless and could turn dangerous any minute. But I couldn't bring myself to stop him, to stop us. I felt defeated on some level. This blitzkrieg love of ours had a firm hold on me. And I allowed myself to be held.

. . .

The cemetery was pretty empty when we got there. I had a vague idea where the tombs were, but we looked in the roster and got directions.

I'd never liked cemeteries. They're so trimmed and bathed in light during the day, looking deceivingly like places of peace. Places of rest, almost kind. Almost welcoming. It was a lie as far as I was concerned. The image that suited the cemetery was that of night, with long and creepy shadows crawling over the ground and dark nooks and crannies. This was where so many people's sorrow and loss gathered, like a wound. I could taste all that sorrow as it simmered through the air. I liked the idea of incineration and having my ashes scattered somewhere. It would leave my loved ones with no physical place to connect to my death, to the hollow I'd left in their lives. Assuming I'd have loved ones. But everyone had someone, didn't they? There was always someone to suffer for our disappearance. This place was a lie. There was no resting place for my mom, and I sure as hell hoped there'd be no resting place for my father. He didn't deserve to rest. What he deserved was to rot in hell and suffer for his heinous crimes: killing my mother and killing a good chunk of me.

Anthony kept pulling at his shirt, at his suit jacket. He looked beautiful, like he always did. Strong and beautiful, and he was all mine. At least for now. I refused to fall victim to custom, so no pretty dress for me. Instead, I was wearing a casual pair of jeans and a shirt. It was too bright for night people, so I had my shades on. A girl always needs her shades.

My parents' stones were near a tree. It was one of those rich trees, vibrant green and with a thick trunk. I wondered how big its roots were, if they spread around wide enough to touch the graves around it. For a silly moment, I imagined it poking at my father's resting place, inflicting well-deserved payback on him by giving his spot no rest. The image made me shudder, and I acknowledged once again the terrible truth, that I was his daughter too. That a part of him lived inside me, that a tentacle of the monster he'd cradled in his soul might have reached inside me. Might have spawned a tiny little monster just waiting to pounce. I was terrified of that most of all. And it froze the blood in my veins to think that maybe I'd be capable of causing harm to those I loved too. Because I was his daughter.

The stones were small, twin granite things declaring their names. My mom's had a generic "loving mother, she will be missed" slogan scribbled on it. It didn't mean much, didn't speak about her at all. But how could a few words speak about my mother? I'd need a novel to do her justice. A few words, a slab of granite, and resting beside the monster who'd killed her. Resting beside the monster she'd never been able to let go of, to walk out on. I ignored the grave of my father and knelt before my mom's stone. Anthony put a white rose beside me on the ground and I picked it up, settled it on her stone. I shook all over, my skin prickled up, and I felt cold. So very cold. Did she feel cold down there? Did she feel lonely? I choked on a strangled cry and set my forehead down against the slab of granite.

I don't know how long I stayed there and cried. My face felt swollen up, my eyes stung, and it was hours later when I got up. Anthony stood there, head bent. His eyebrows sagged. I walked into him, pushing my forehead into his chest. He didn't move.

"Thank you," I whispered.

"Can I hug you?"

I choked into his tie. "Yes, please."

His arms closed around my shivering body, and he squeezed me tight. The harder he held me the lighter my heart felt. I danced on that edge between fear and pleasure, between fear and delight. He took me there with just one caress, with his taste and the touch of his body. They were imprinted in my brain. My body sagged into his embrace and I took a deep, shuddering breath.

"You'll have to drag me back into the car. I don't have it in me to walk on my own."

He bent over me and kissed the top of my head.

"It's okay, sparrow. I've got you. You don't have to do it on your own."

Those words sank into me and took residence in the pit of my soul. I liked that idea. It was scary and new, but I liked it. For however long it lasted, I didn't have to make it on my own. I could lean on him. I could go weak in the knees, and he'd carry me if I wanted him to.

On the ride back I turned on the radio. Adele sang at me again, all that tumult and beauty filling my soul. For a moment there it felt overfull, but I welcomed the sensation. It beat feeling empty. I'd take overfull over empty any day. Anthony's hand crawled into my lap, and he closed his strong fingers over my open palm. His eyes remained fixed on the road, and I stared at him. At his profile, at his ears. He had sexy ears. I'd never thought of ears as sexy before, but here they were. Sexy.

"I want you to stay with me," I found myself saying.

He turned around, inspected my face. His hand closed tighter around mine but his eyes returned to the road. "You mean today?"

I shook my head. "Today, tomorrow…for as long as you can put up with a broken thing like me."

"You're not broken, sparrow. You're just scarred. We're all scarred. It means we survived things that hurt. It doesn't make us broken. It makes us strong."

I smiled. "Ever the optimist, huh?"

"I'll be whatever you want me to be. Whatever you'd like me to be. As long as I can stay."

I closed my other hand over our joined ones and caressed his wrist with the tips of my fingers. "We're such a cliché, aren't we? The sexy dancer and her boss, hooking up."

He laughed. "We're not 'hooking up.' We're in love. That's not a cliché, sparrow."

"People might start to think you've got a thing for birds, you know?"

"Let them think whatever they'd like. They will anyway."

I settled back into the seat, looked at the scenery as it flashed by us. "Anthony?"

"Yeah."

"You might pull me out of the dark woods I'm lost in. Not right away, maybe not tomorrow. But there will be this morning, sometime in the future, this awesome day. I'll wake up, look at you and hear you snoring and—"

"Slander and calumny! I don't snore."

"Pffft, baby, you snore like a grizzly bear roaring for food after months of hibernating."

"I do not snore."

I sighed. "You're completely ruining my moment. And you do snore."

"Do not."

"Do too."

He snorted. "Fine. I'll just go with it because you're so determined. But we both know perfectly well that—"

"You snore," I added, grinning.

"Okay," he grumbled. "Just as long as you don't start accusing me of Saggy Butt Syndrome."

"Oh, you'll know when that starts to manifest. You'll see me running away at the speed of light."

He sighed. "You just want me for my looks. I knew it."

"Of course. Though there are other definite perks that go with it."

I grinned and felt a little better as he smiled too. He had this magic power of taking me from one mood and planting me in another. Even better than music or dancing.

"We'll be all right, sparrow. One day at a time."

I nodded. One day at a time sounded good to me, realistic. Finding some magical cure would be impossible. I'd never forget or move on from what had happened two years ago. But maybe with enough practice I could learn to live with it, to function around it. After all, if I gave in and lived in fear I'd only make my father win. His cruelty and viciousness would have prevailed over me as well as over my mom. I didn't want to give him that victory.

"He used to beat her," I mumbled, staring at my knees. "She'd show some bruises now and then, but she always acted like they weren't there. And I felt awkward mentioning them, because she just pretended so hard…I thought maybe I'd make her feel bad if I mentioned them. So I didn't. I pretend they weren't there. I never even tried to pull her out of those dark woods she was lost in. I just pretended they were bright and shiny and had flowers all over."

"Abused spouses are hard to pull out of that darkness. You shouldn't blame yourself. It was her decision to stay."

"I know that. It just makes me so angry."

"It's all right to get angry. I think you're right to be angry. And screw all that forgiving routine some people preach, too. You have a right to never forgive him."

"Did you forgive your sister for not saving herself?"

He flinched, then sighed. Squeezed my hand tighter. "After the first couple of years, yes. Did you forgive your mom?"

I bit my lip, tears threatening to fog up my view. "Yeah. Yeah, I think I did. Sure helps that I do have someone to blame for her death."

He smiled, that usual, humorless smile of his.

"I think your sister would be very proud of you," I said admiring his profile.

He dragged my hand to his lips and kissed it hard. Then he took our mingled hands and set them back in my lap. We drove in silence.

Seven months later…

Mornings were harder than ever. I rarely managed to sleep on my back anymore. It was very disconcerting to wake up and see a wall looming over you, then realize it was your tummy. At least it beat running to the toilet and barfing halfway through every sentence. I did run to the bathroom a lot, anyway. Oh, the joys.

I hadn't been dancing for months. Forget dancing, in fact, I had issues just walking for distances longer than ten yards. But there were bright sides to it. Like Anthony waking me up with a big cup of kiwi and peach ice cream, warm delicious coffee—I'd die before giving that up—and the occasional foot massage. Not a bad thing, all in all.

"Hey, ladies. We've got that appointment today."

"I know," I grumbled.

I hated his talking to me in plural thing. But I did love that ice cream. Short attention span was another one of those recent developments. Big appetite to go with it, though. Had no trouble focusing on the tray balanced on my tummy.

"I want some orange juice or something citrusy. We have any?"

He chuckled. "Coming right up."

Well, I did want some orange juice. But mostly I wanted to dig into that ice cream and then sip coffee. Maybe some pastries? I groaned. By the time he came back with the juice, I'd forgotten about the pastries. I threw back about half the glass and launched back into the ice cream.

"Than you," I mumbled around the spoon.

He pulled it slowly out of my mouth. "You were saying?"

I blushed. "Thank you."

He smiled and went all doe-eyed. *Men.*

"You're getting a kick out of this, aren't you? Playing daddy and all."

"Well, I am going to be a daddy soon. I need the practice."

I rolled my eyes. "You're lucky my ankles hurt too bad for me to make a run for it."

He chuckled and leaned toward the foot of the bed, massaging my ankles. I groaned and closed my eyes. "God, that feels divine."

"Whatever I can do for you, it's my pleasure."

I nibbled on my lip. "How about taking the tray back down so I can get a shower?"

He reached down and kissed my forehead then left, humming. He was getting such a kick out of this.

• • •

I stared at the little doll on the screen. She looked a lot like Anthony and vaguely like me. Very vaguely. Of course, I wouldn't admit that unless seriously tortured. My official story was my baby looked exactly like me and I stuck to it. Anthony's hold on my hand grew firmer. His heart beat so hard I felt it pulse into the palm of his hand. You'd think he was the one carrying the baby, not me.

"She looks just like you," he murmured.

I frowned. "Of course she looks just like me. We're going to have to hire a team of bodyguards when she hits puberty, she's that gorgeous."

The doc chuckled. "I think it might be too early to figure out who she looks the most like. But she's your kid—she looks like both of you."

Anthony blinked hard. He always got more emotional about these things than I did. I was partly too freaked out by the notion of becoming a mom to get too squishy over the whole process. And terrified of the idea that the baby would eventually have to come out. Not a happy prospect as far as technicalities went. Plus thinking about having a baby in my arms sometime soon sort of gave me a panic attack. It was a good kind of freak out though, not the ugly kind I used to have.

I reached out toward the screen and ran my fingers over the small face there. Would she look like my mom at all? Would she have the same eyes I got from her, or that same shape of lips? Maybe the same cheekbones, or the same big waves of dark brown hair. I wanted her to have something of my mom, something of her grandmother. But then I thought maybe she'd have something of my father too, and that scared me. Anthony's dark eyes were good contenders too. And his cleft chin for sure. Maybe his dimples as well. I loved his dimples.

Whoever she'd take after, I solemnly swore again to keep my baby safe. From everyone, from anyone. From me, if I had to. I solemnly swore I'd never allow anything to hurt her, to break her heart. And I knew as I thought it that I'd never be able to actually defend her from the world. But I'd make sure she could defend herself, that she'd be strong and brave. The little shape under my fingertips gave me such a bundle of contradicting emotions.

"Hey, Melissa," I whispered. "Mommy and Daddy are making your room beautiful for you. If Daddy ever manages to assemble the crib."

He cleared his throat. "I know how to assemble it, sparrow. I just didn't want it to know I knew. It'll be a sneaky assembly attack."

The doc and I laughed as Anthony's cheeks colored. He took that very seriously. The crib was standing there in his old guest bedroom, a pile of wood and enough instructions to fly a rocket. Anthony kept trying to figure it out and failing. He also refused any help. He was going overboard with the daddy thing already, and our baby girl wasn't even born yet. But it was something he needed to do. I just poked fun at his stubbornness now and then. He'd either break down and let me help him or put the thing together, finally. Both outcomes were all right by me. Anthony was an amazing man and I loved him, but he couldn't read and follow instructions if his life depended on it. Not unless I was giving the instructions. Those he managed to follow so beautifully it was art. Our relationship was a delicate balance, but where it worked it was magnificent.

I looked down at my swollen belly and wondered if I was insane for doing this whole thing. I had to be. But then again, I thought you had to be a little insane to be brave, to take risks. Having a kid was the most insane thing I could imagine. It took endless amounts of bravery.

When we got home with our new baby pic, I went and set it in the nursery. The walls were a soft beige. It relaxed me. Part of the furniture was already up, beautiful cream and light green. The pile of to-be-crib was close to the last part we had to get done, then I'd move on decorating to the walls. I didn't like bare walls—they depressed me no matter how beautiful their color was. I rubbed my belly as I looked around.

"Sparrow, your phone's ringing."

I sighed and walked to the living room. My cell was more of a home phone at the moment, I just kept forgetting to carry it around with me like I used to. My ankles felt stiff as I went down the stairs. Each time I had to go up or down on those things I thought of moving back into my old apartment. But we didn't have enough room there. I sub-rented it to the new dancer at Satine because the idea of giving it up bugged me.

Of course by the time I got to the phone it had stopped ringing. I hated when that happened. The screen showed Doug's number so I called back.

"Hey, dolls."

I sighed. "I always wonder if you mean I'm the size of two dolls or if you're talking to my baby and me both when you say that. To my *unborn* baby."

"You're beautiful, Bea. Don't you worry about that."

I snorted. "Of course I am. But I'm also unable to see my feet. That particular joy I fully wish upon you."

"Hey, now, don't go surly on me."

"I'm pregnant. I can do whatever I want and get away with it. Seriously. Yesterday I went into a store, tore into a chocolate I hadn't paid for and the sales-chick just smiled at me all doe-eyed. I think I could rob a bank. Nobody would stop me, they'd just smile like goofballs and think I'm craving dollar bills."

I heard Anthony laugh in the kitchen and Doug laughed too. It was easy to laugh. Men were so oblivious to the shocking power of the belly.

"Justine and I wanted to drop by. You guys did an ultrasound today, right? We wanna see the little girl."

I scoffed. "She looks like a sea-creature in there. I'm not sure I wanna make these pictures public."

"Come on, doll. I'll bring you something good if you say yes."

I grinned. My plan all along. "I want some meatball spaghetti from Lucia's. And cake from MariBell's. And fruit tarts. Many, many fruit tarts. Then I'll consider it."

Doug gulped. "Sure. We'll be…right over."

I grinned and settled into the sofa after we hung up. Lucia's was virtually impossible to get into, and MariBell's had lines the size of the Atlantic Ocean. I rubbed the belly and set my feet up on the coffee table.

Justine and Doug had a weird thing going on. They ate each other up through glances but insisted they weren't a couple. They did show up together, leave together, and have a peculiar amount of common stories to tell when we got together. Maybe they were just friends for now, but I could totally see that evolving. They were awesome friends, always knew to bring me food. Usually did a quicker job at it than others might. But it would be a couple hours before they could get the yummy stuff no matter how good they were.

"You're getting a kick out of this, aren't you?"

I looked up to see Anthony bringing over some peach and kiwi ice cream. My mouth watered. God, I loved the man. And the ice cream. Mostly in that order.

"Have I told you lately how much I love you?"

He gave me my newest drug—the ice cream—and smiled. "You're just trying to get into my fridge," he said with a glint in his eyes.

I groaned as I dug into the creamy, fruity deliciousness. Nothing had ever tasted so good to me. I never was big on food, but God how I loved it lately.

"I'm teaching Melissa the basic principles of life. You want, you get, you enjoy. It's a major life lesson," I said around a mouthful.

He sat down beside my feet on the coffee table and slowly rubbed his way from my ankles up to my knees. That was pure bliss. I leaned my head back, eyes closed. Pure bliss.

"Have you thought about what I asked you?" he asked softly.

I cracked open my eyes and got my head back up to peer at him. "You're taking advantage of my moment of weakness, aren't you?"

His hands worked around my feet and made me sigh in delight. "You want, you get, you enjoy. Isn't that what you said?" he said grinning.

I rolled my eyes. "You're getting way too full of yourself. Did you put the crib together yet?"

He cringed but kept massaging my feet. I sighed and set my head back against the touch, eyes closed.

"I'm thinking about it, Anthony. I am. I don't know why a piece of paper is that important to you. We're together regardless."

"True. But then, if it's so not important, why not get it done?"

I snorted and rolled my eyes. The idea of marriage scared the beejesus out of me. A lot worse than having a kid, in fact. I couldn't deal with both of those things at the same time.

"I'll think about it. But don't expect a straight answer for at least three months."

"Why three?"

"I'm guessing after Melissa is born I'll be willing to say yes to anything just to get more sleep in the morning."

He chuckled. "My baby girl will help me out, I know she will."

I opened my eyes and stared at the ceiling. "I was a vicious baby, you know? Mom used to tell me I'd wake up in the middle of the night and bellow without mercy unless she'd rock me, walk around the house carrying me, and sing at the same time. I'm scared to think Melissa might be just like me."

"She'll be perfect if she's just like you," he said softly.

"So you'll do that whole gig if she'll be like that?"

"Of course."

Yeah, the doe-eyed stare. It worked miracles. I grinned and closed my eyes. He kept massaging my feet.

"I love you, Beatrice Stevens. Though I think Beatrice Gowl sounds better."

"Love you too. But don't push your luck," I mumbled.

I wasn't fixed, not by a long shot. Maybe I'd never be fixed. But I was strong and brave. Looking at Anthony I realized my life had already turned out way better than I'd ever dared to hope. I had this awesome guy on my side, ready to hold my hand and bring me ice cream at three in the morning if I so desired. His eyes lit up when he looked at me and the belly, and I just felt it in my heart he loved us both. I could only hope that it would be enough to build a good future on. Because I sure as hell loved him to pieces. And the thought I carried this little miracle inside me, this little doll we'd brought into existence—it almost filled my eyes with tears.

Somehow my happy ending had found me, even if the road had been bumpy. I had worked for it, it belonged to me. To us. Our happy ending.

I might even marry Anthony someday, I was that happy.

About the Author

Livia Olteano is a loud and proud coffee addict, lover of all things beautiful, and incurable romantic.

She believes stories are the best kind of magic there is. And life would be horrible without magic. Her hobbies include losing herself in the minds and souls of characters, giving up countless nights of sleep to get to know said characters, and trying to introduce them to the world. Sometimes they appreciate her efforts. The process would probably go quicker if they'd bring her a cup of coffee now and then when stopping by. Characters—what can you do, right?

Stop by *www.liviaolteano.com* for the latest news and rants of glory.

A Sneak Peek from Crimson Romance
(From *Trusting Again* by Peggy Bird)

"I love it when she has the men in the audience sing the chorus to 'Eight Miles Wide,'" Liz Fairchild said. "Hearing deep voices sing about the size of their vaginas never fails to amuse me."

Cynthia Blaine had known Liz for years and, although she wasn't surprised by anything the other woman said, she was sometimes still astonished by where Liz chose to say it. However, shushing her was a waste of effort. So was pointing out the startled expressions of the people who'd heard the comment. Liz had never learned to care about keeping her voice down or her opinion to herself.

"You like saying that out loud, don't you?" Cynthia said.

"No one objects to that word anymore, do they? And if they do, maybe it'll clear out the place so we can get a table. Otherwise, we're out of luck. The bar's full," Liz said.

They'd just come from a matinee of the Oregon Symphony featuring Storm Large, a performer with a great voice and an amazing repertoire of songs, not all of which were appropriate for the faint of heart, a category which included Liz's favorite, her signature song. Now, standing at the entrance to the Heathman Hotel bar, the women were hoping to find a table so they could have a glass of wine.

This girls' afternoon out also included Amanda St. Claire, who was doing a recon for a table in the back. Amanda hadn't been out much since the birth of her baby and Liz, whose art gallery exhibited both Amanda's art glass and Cynthia's designer jewelry, had, as she described it, "arranged the excursion to rectify that."

Amanda rejoined them just in time to catch the last part of the conversation. "It's full there, too," she said waving toward the other room. "There are three empty chairs at a table for four, but there was a guy sitting there. I guess he's waiting for people to join him."

"Did you ask?" Liz said.

"No, it seemed rude."

"If he has the only empty chairs in the place, it's not rude. If you can't do it, I will." Liz headed to the area that served as overflow bar, tearoom, and place to lunch for the hotel restaurant.

In a few minutes, she reappeared in the door to the back room and motioned to the other two to join her.

"Oh, my God. Did we get lucky," she said in a low voice. "And not just by scoring a table. The man we'll be sitting with is one of the most beautiful creatures ever to walk the planet."

"So, Liz, when did you say Collins will be back in Portland?" Amanda asked, trailing behind Cynthia.

"I didn't and you're usually more subtle than that. I love Collins but I'm not blind. You'll understand when you see this man," Liz said. "And to answer your question, however rhetorical it may have been, this is his week in Portland. He should be home now. With any luck, he'll even have dinner—"

"Holy hell." Cynthia stopped so suddenly, Amanda ran into the back of her. "Is that the guy you're talking about?" She nodded toward a man sitting alone at a table for four, a glass of red wine in his hand.

"Yup, isn't he gorgeous?" Liz asked.

"I know him," Cynthia said. "He commissioned a piece of my jewelry a month or so ago for his girlfriend."

"Damn. There goes my plan to set you up. I figured I might find a way for Amanda and me to leave without you so he'd ask you to dinner."

"Don't you dare do anything like that," Cynthia said, raising her voice slightly and emphasizing the "dare" part of the sentence. The last thing she needed was Liz's heavy-handed matchmaking. It was uncomfortable enough when Liz tried to fix her up with one of her artists. Cynthia definitely didn't want any attempts to get her together with this man.

Not when he woke up a hatch of butterflies in her stomach every time she thought about him. Ever since he'd walked into the Erickson Gallery, she'd been full of fluttery things on a regular basis. As she was now.

She smoothed the skirt of her plain lavender linen maxi dress, trying to get rid of the wrinkles, then tied the ends of the deep purple shrug she wore over it a little tighter around her waist. It was too late to wish she'd worn something sexier. Or had put her tawny blonde hair up in some intricate roll, rather than a simple braid down the middle of her back. Worn fuck-me shoes instead of the flat sandals she had on. Put on a little more make-up; put on any make-up at all.

Oh, for God's sake. Wearing something else wouldn't have made any difference. He has a girlfriend. One he spent big bucks on for a birthday present. And what the hell was she thinking, anyway? Even if he wasn't attached, he was way out of her league. After the whole Josh disaster last year, she'd vowed never to get herself in a similar situation again. She'd barely gotten out of that relationship with any shred of ego intact.

As the three women approached the table, the subject of her fantasies stood to greet them. Cynthia was sure his picture was in the dictionary next to the phrase "tall, dark, and handsome." Cliché it may be but, in his case, true. He was well over six feet tall, with skin the color of a latte, and thick, black-brown hair that curled around his ears and at the back of his neck. The first time she'd seen him in Seattle, she'd immediately wanted to thread her fingers through that hair. Lick up the side of his neck until she got to his jaw line, an earlobe, his full-lipped mouth, whatever she could reach to kiss. Put her arms over those broad shoulders. Earn one of those sensuous smiles.

Everything about the man was burned into her brain including what was, she was pretty sure from watching it walk away from her, the best ass in the Northwest. So she knew if she wasn't careful, before this little unexpected encounter in Portland had ended, she'd likely be drooling all over him like a St. Bernard.

When the man recognized Cynthia, a broad grin spread over his face and lit up his brown eyes. "If I'd known you were one of the women who were table-less, I'd have carried it out to you. With a bottle of champagne."

"So, the birthday gift was a success," Cynthia said.

"Absolutely," he said. "It was the hit of the evening. I've been out of town on business or I would have let you know how much my friend appreciated it." He turned the smile on the other two women. "Sorry. Didn't mean to be rude. I'm Marius Hernandez. Cynthia created an amazing piece of jewelry for me to give a friend as a birthday present."

"This is Liz Fairchild, Marius. She has a gallery in Portland where I have some of my work. And this is Amanda St. Claire. She shows her work at The Fairchild, too."

"Everyone knows Amanda St. Claire's art glass. And I've read about your gallery, Liz. I don't know what I've done to deserve the pleasure of three beautiful and talented women joining me but whatever it was, I hope I do it often." He gestured toward the table. "Please. Sit. Let me flag down a server and get you something to drink."

Liz took the chair next to Marius and Amanda sat opposite her, leaving the place across from him for Cynthia. She moved the chair back from the table a bit, sure that if he went back to the slouch he'd been in before he stood, she'd be brushing knees with him and she didn't think she could handle that.

But instead of inhabiting the chair with a casual sprawl, he sat up straighter, his forearms on the table in front of him which put her hands, not her knees, in danger. Even without touching him,

Cynthia was unnerved by being this close to him. She played with the strap of the shoulder bag in her lap, twisting her fingers in it, trying not to watch him. But she wasn't able to keep herself from sneaking peeks at him out of the corner of her eye.

"Cyn, what do you want?" Amanda's voice broke through the heated mist that had obscured every other thought as soon as she'd seen Marius. "We've ordered our drinks and some food to share. The server's waiting for you."

"Sorry, a glass of house red, please."

"Make that a bottle of the Malbec I'm drinking," Marius said to the server before asking Cynthia, "Is that okay with you? I'm drinking red wine, too, and with you and Liz ordering red, it makes sense to have a bottle."

"I've never had a Malbec," she said, "but sure. Sounds fine."

"Most Northwesterners who drink red wine stick to local pinot noirs. But this is one of my favorites. It's from Argentina, from a high altitude vineyard in the Andes. I think you'll like it."

"So, Marius, now that we have that settled," Liz began, clearly finished with the wine discussion, "I'd love to know more about you. You commissioned a piece from Cynthia in Seattle, but are hanging out in Portland. Do you live in Washington or Oregon? Or do you slide back and forth across the Columbia at will?"

He seemed to take Liz in stride, merely smiling at her as he answered. "I live in Seattle. I'm in Portland for a coffee convention."

"There are conventions for coffee?" Liz said. "Who knew?"

"Coffee's big business. Especially now that Starbucks has taken it out of the supermarket and made it gourmet. My family has been in the business for several generations and we've seen the change. Benefited from it, to be honest."

"You sell coffee?" Liz asked.

"Not in the sense I think you mean. We're brokers for coffee plantation owners in Central America. We arrange the deals between coffee roasters here and plantations there."

"Coffee roasters like Starbucks?"

"Don't I wish. No, we have several dozen clients in and around Portland, same in Seattle, and a growing number in California."

"Is your family in Seattle?" Amanda asked.

"Miami. My family came from Cuba when Castro took over." Before Liz could ask another question, he went on, "My grandfather started the business. My father and uncles run it now and my brother, a cousin, and I are next in line. I was sent to Seattle to open a West Coast office to handle all the business your coffee culture was bringing us. It's only me, a couple computers, and an assistant but…" His self-deprecating smile didn't really match the rest of his confident body language.

Which was what Cynthia was staring at—his body. Especially his shoulders. His gorgeous shoulders were clad in a jacket that never wrinkled when he moved, like it was part of his skin. She was sure he had his suits made for him. The one he wore today was brown, the perfect complement to his milky-coffee skin. The fabric looked expensive, imported from someplace like Italy. His cream-colored shirt had French cuffs held together with chunky gold cuff links. She wanted to touch the fabric of the shirt; it looked so soft, so smooth. Maybe it was silk, like his tie, which she thought was Prada.

What the hell was wrong with her? First obsessing about her clothes, now his? What men wore had never been of any interest to her. Women's clothes barely held her attention for more than the ten minutes it took for her to throw on jeans and a T-shirt every morning. She had to pull herself together. Liz and Amanda were having a normal conversation with this man while she sat like a lump, too busy thinking about things like his clothes—or what was under them—to say anything, much less anything intelligent.

"I guess you must find Seattle a bit of a change from Miami," Amanda was saying when Cynthia tuned back into the conversation.

"You have no idea. Just about everything's different, from the weather to people's idea of fun to the politics. I've gotten to like it now. Except for the beaches. Even after two years, I still miss Florida beaches."

The wine arrived; he tasted and approved it. The conversation went on, mostly around Cynthia not with her. She'd made some progress toward normalcy—she'd stopped obsessing about his clothes. Now, she was intent on making sure no part of her body touched any part of his. When he handed her a glass of wine, she took it without coming in contact with his hand. She kept her knees clenched tightly together and primly set to the side of her chair so there was no chance they would brush his. She avoided eye contact.

But the one thing she couldn't get away from was the smell of his aftershave or cologne or, who knows, maybe pheromones, wafting across the table. He smelled like some exotic spice she couldn't name. She had never, in her entire life, smelled anything that good. It was irresistible. Like every other part of him was, from the crown of his head to the just-got-out-of-bed dark stubble on his cheeks and jaw that would feel wonderfully scratchy on her skin. From the body under that custom-made suit she'd stopped thinking about until now, when she started thinking about it again, to his voice that was like a good piece of music, deep and resonant, layered with meaning. And his eyes, oh God, his eyes …

"Cyn, is something wrong? You're so quiet." Amanda sounded concerned.

Before she could answer, Cynthia caught the expression on Marius's face. Damn. He knew exactly why she was quiet, why she was sitting like some well-behaved schoolgirl. It seemed those brown eyes could see into her heart and soul.

"I was thinking about a new piece I'm working on. Sorry."

He raised an eyebrow and buried his half-smile in his glass of wine.

"Is this for my gallery or are you going to waste it on that place in Seattle where you still have your work?" Liz asked.

"It's a commission that came from Max's gallery, that place where the owner has been as good to me in Seattle as you've been to me in Portland. And didn't I just bring you my Victorian neckpieces no one else has seen?"

"I guess I'll take that as some sort of atonement for giving him your Cleopatra collars first. Not that anyone in Seattle would ever appreciate anything like that."

A Cleopatra collar was exactly what Marius had commissioned from her, but demonstrating he was as smart as he was sexy, he only winked at her and stayed out of the discussion.

The conversation moved on to subjects less likely to make her discomfited. In response to his questions, Amanda explained to Marius some of the fine points of kiln-formed glass art. In return, he answered hers about coffee buying. In her usual outrageously flirty manner, Liz encouraged him to come to her gallery before he returned to Seattle. Cynthia said little unless prompted by her friends and even then made only brief comments, still tongue-tied by sitting across from him.

An hour later, Marius glanced at an expensive-looking watch, re-buttoned the top button of his shirt, tightened his tie and apologized for having to leave for a business dinner. Before he left, he shook the hand of each of the three women, seeming to linger with Cynthia longer than with the other two. At least it felt like he lingered, taking her smaller hand between both of his, holding it in what felt more like the clasp of a lover's hand than a good-bye handshake. She noticed, as she had when they first met, that in spite of the beautiful clothes, he had calluses on his hands that could only come from some kind of physical work. It added an aspect to him that fascinated her even more.

She hoped he hadn't noticed how her hand trembled when he held it.

• • •

Marius couldn't believe his luck. He'd been trying to find a way to get back to the Erickson Gallery for weeks so he could do what he should have done when he'd picked up the gift for a family friend—ask the beautiful artist who'd made the piece to have dinner with him. But he'd been traveling on business for most of the past month, ending up in Portland, where he'd been bored and counting the days until he could get back to Seattle.

Until he decided to kill time before his dinner meeting with a glass of wine. And there she was.

In only two brief encounters, Cynthia Blaine had managed to intrigue him. Curvy where most of the women he'd met lately had been long and lean, her face was clean of make-up, her eyes clear of calculation about what his net worth might be. He had his pick of arm candy, but going to dinner with women who were conventionally beautiful, fashionably dressed, and often more ambitious than he was—which was saying quite a lot—had worn thin. Not that he was looking for a long-term commitment. But someone real seemed like a nice change. And Cynthia Blaine was that—real and talented and beautiful.

When he'd first met her, he'd thought she was equally attracted. But he had wondered if she'd written him off because he was obviously buying a piece of expensive jewelry for a woman even though he kept emphasizing it was for a *friend*, hoping she'd get the inference. Today he thought the message must have gotten through. The way she'd flushed when he smiled at her, held her body back from touching him, looked away so he wouldn't know she'd been staring at him all seemed to say she felt the same attraction.

What he hadn't been able to do was cut her out of her herd of friends without being too obvious or obnoxious. So, he scribbled a note on the back of a business card and left it with the server when he had the bill for the women's drinks charged to his room. She assured him she'd get it to the woman in the purple dress with the long braid.

• • •

Marius was barely out the door before Liz turned on her friend.

"Cynthia, what the hell is wrong with you? Why didn't you tell us about him?"

"Why would I tell you about him? He was just another customer," she replied. "Can I have the last bit of that cheese?" She reached for the plate. Liz pushed it out of her reach.

"Don't change the subject. How could you not think we'd be interested in one of the most handsome men ever put on this earth?"

"Don't be ridiculous." She tried for the cheese plate again. And failed, thanks to Liz's determination. "I just sold him a neckpiece for his girlfriend."

"The girlfriend part, I grant you, is a shame. But, my God, girl, just run down the list of the other virtues: killer good-looking, charming, polite, interested in what we have to say, willing to ignore phone calls while he talked to us, the good taste and money to commission work from you and buy that suit. What's not worth talking about on that list?"

"I guess I wasn't paying attention."

Liz snorted. "Right. You were stunned into silence just sitting across from him."

"No, I wasn't."

"Don't bother, petal. No one will believe you. It was too obvious. Not that I blame you. You could drown in those eyes. And his smile gave me some idea of what it'll feel like when I get old enough to have hot flashes." She fanned herself to make her point more obvious.

"Did you notice his hands?" Amanda asked. "I love the way he talks with them. They're so big and graceful. I bet he could palm a basketball with them."

Cynthia's hand was still trembling from the handshake. Oh, yeah, she'd noticed his hands all right.

"A basketball? Honey, he could palm anything I have with them," Liz said. As the other two women burst into giggles, she added, "Please don't repeat that in front of Collins. He doesn't have much of a sense of humor when I make comments like that."

A half hour later, Liz went to pay the bill and learned that Marius had taken care of it, adding one more item to her list of reasons Marius Hernandez was God's gift to the world. The three women parted at the parking garage across the street from the concert venue, Liz headed for Southwest Portland where the man she lived with waited; Amanda to Northeast Portland, her husband and her new baby, and Cynthia for the freeway back to Seattle.

• • •

The dinner hostess at the Heathman always rearranged the desk to suit the way she liked things before she started her shift. Tonight, while she was moving things around, she found a business card with a note written on the back. No one seemed to know who it was for or why it was there. She pitched it into the recycling.

In the mood for more Crimson Romance?
Check out *His Fantasy Maid*
by Susan Blexrud
at *CrimsonRomance.com*.